MW01128191

July Culler

A
Novel
By
Ron Charles

To Terry,
Another time,
Another place.
Hope this takes
you there.
Ron Charles

6/3/14

C & C Books
Los Angeles

Acknowledgement

I would like to thank my wonderful wife Gayle, who after years of hearing my stories about this, encouraged me to write this book and helped me tremendously in editing and preparing it for publication.

I would also like to thank our old friend and extraordinary artist, Charlie Brown, for doing the beautiful art work on the cover.

Foreword

This is the story of a very unusual and unlikely friendship. Because of the social attitudes of that time and place and the differences in age and circumstances, it was unlikely that these two would ever have even met.

In telling the story, the narrative is the voice of the man and his observations looking back at the time of his childhood. Only when the writer is quoted as a young boy, is he speaking as he did at that age. Hopefully, it gives the reader a window to an unusual time and a rare situation.

This book is a novel and as such, would of course have to be called fiction, because some parts have been omitted, others added and enhanced or enlarged upon to give the story continuity and make it work as a dramatic piece. Also, some names have been changed, others have not.

To paraphrase Thomas Wolfe in his message, "To The Reader" in his novel, "Look Homeward Angel" :

"Fiction is not fact, but fiction is fact selected and understood, fiction is fact arranged and charged with purpose. A novelist may use memories of half the people in a town to make a single character in his novel. This is not the whole method, but the writer believes it illustrates the method in a novel that is written from the distance of years and is without rancor or bitter intent."

For Gayle

1.

I suppose we heard that they were coming about three or four
months before we ever saw any of them. The closer it got to
spring and then summer, the more we heard about them and what it
would be like to have them there. Nothing like this had ever
happened there before. Everybody was going to have to be
careful.

This was a coal town and coal mining was the all consuming and
most important thing that turned the wheels and made the money.
Things were old and rugged in this place - the mountains that made
the coal and the generations of people who had lived and worked
there. Life was hard and attitudes were slow in changing.

Except for the internal combustion engine and the model T Ford,
which changed the world and led to the trucks that hauled the coal,
not much had changed there in a very long time.

The plan was to widen and improve the road up Slate Creek.

That meant they would have to blast out huge chunks of mountain rock and dirt before they could even begin on the road itself. The creek and the road beside it were at the bottom of a very deep and very narrow valley.

The creek followed the floor of the valley like a snake and there were some places where there wasn't room for much more than the creek and the road, the coal mines tucked back in the hollows and a little space for a few houses, all of which were covered with a thick layer of coal dust.

Coal dust was everywhere, to some degree or other. You breathed it, drank it in your water and ate it in your food. It was in your hair, on your skin and in your eyes. It was just a fact of life that you had to deal with, if you lived there.

The word was that the road job might take a year or two to finish. One of the main reasons for building the new road was to make it

3.

better for the huge trucks that were constantly hauling the coal from the mines to the coal tipples, where it was loaded into railroad cars. These were ten wheel tandem trucks - two sets of tandem wheels on each side in the back and two wheels in the front.

You could feel a rumble under your feet before you could even see them coming around a curve and a second or two after they passed, the trail of coal grit that followed all of them, hit you in the face.

They carried fifteen to twenty tons of coal per load, so they had already pretty well destroyed the old road. After all these years, they had quite simply, beaten it to death. The potholes were cavernous and besides that, the old road wasn't wide enough for the trucks and regular traffic to pass safely. Whenever there was a confrontation between a truck and a car, the car always lost. There had been a lot of accidents.

4.

But it wasn't just the road that was heavy on their minds. It was who was going to build it. The ominous thing that people were worrying and wondering about was the road gang. They had seen road gangs before. There was nothing unusual about that, but this was different. This road gang was going to be made up entirely of convicts - black convicts - on a chain gang.

In most parts of the south, in the late forties, that wouldn't have been even slight cause for pause. Half the roads in that part of the country had been built by black convicts. In this case, however, it was a big event and the cause of months of discussion and speculation. It was important because there wasn't a black person living in the entire county and hadn't been for as long as anybody could remember.

I was only eleven that summer, but I can still remember hearing people say with pride, "They ain't no niggers in this county and there never will be." Of course, not everyone felt that way toward

5.

black people. To be sure, there were many who didn't, but there

were plenty who did. The ones who did, seemed to think that

black people in general were chomping at the bit to live there.

The closer the time came, the more talk there was about the safety

of the women and the fact that the road was to be rebuilt that

passed right in front of the big consolidated school, which housed

grades one through twelve. There were twelve to thirteen hundred

kids from all over the county who went to school there every day

and most of them, who ranged in age from six to eighteen, had

never even seen a black person. They only knew what they had

been told.

It was as though the kids were waiting to see alien creatures from

another planet. They didn't know what to expect. They only knew

that it was supposed to be really bad.

When the convicts finally got there, they spent the first couple of weeks building a camp, a sort of tent city, with shotgun guards. The camp was beside a curve in Slate Creek called, "Bend of Slate". The guards would drive the men three or four miles to and from work everyday in large trucks.

It was a hot, dusty summer and they had started work on the new road right across the creek from my house. I used to sit on the back porch and watch the men work. I felt really privileged to have something as exciting as this going on so close to home.

I noticed right away that there were differences in the way they treated certain prisoners. Some were in chains, hands and feet, and heavily guarded. Others weren't in chains, but they were also under heavy guard. Then there were still others, only a few, who had no chains and no guards.

These few were allowed to move around fairly freely, but they were never, ever allowed out of sight. They didn't have to work as hard as the other men either. The work was back breaking. The job for most of the men was digging with picks and shovels and breaking up huge rocks with sledge hammers, then hauling the rubble away in wheelbarrows, to dump it where they were told. That would be hard enough even without chains.

With chains, it seemed almost impossible, but they did it eight or so hours a day, for weeks, months, years on end. When the judge sentenced them to "hard labor", this was what he had in mind and the guards seemed to enjoy making it as hard as possible. You had to be strong just to survive it.

For the first day or two, I was content to sit on the back porch and whittle and watch. After that, I finally got up enough nerve to get a little closer. The creek usually dried up about mid summer, so it was pretty low by this time. Most summers, after it had dried up, my buddies and I would go snake hunting under the rocks in the creek bed. But this year the snakes got a break, because of the road gang. I just walked across on rocks that were sticking up out of the shallow water. Had to be careful though, some of the rocks were still slick.

The first guard that saw me when I climbed up the bank on the other side, told me to stay back. He looked gigantic to me. A huge fat man with a big round belly hanging over his belt, a big wad of chewing tobacco in his cheek and a twelve gauge shotgun cradled in his arms. I stood a few feet behind him and watched for awhile. When I tried to get a little closer, he warned me again, "Boy, stay away from them niggers - they'll kill you." That scared me for awhile.

So, for another day or so, I would only go as far as the guard. But, the convicts didn't look as mean as he said they were - not to me anyway. I kept pestering the guard with questions, which he grudgingly answered. Little by little, I got him to explain why only a few of the men were allowed to move around freely.

He said they were "trustees". I asked him what "trustee" meant and he said it meant that they got special privileges because they had "behaved themselves" for a long time. From the way he said it, I got the impression that he meant they had "behaved" for a lot of years.

Later that night, while my mother and I were having dinner or supper, as they called it in the south in those days, she asked me if I had been over where the convicts were. I started to tell her that I had, but I decided not to.

"Nope. Just watched 'em from across the creek, that's all." She gave me a long look to see if I was telling the truth. I couldn't tell whether she quite believed me or not. "Well, you stay away from those men." she said. "They're dangerous." I just nodded. She just kept looking at me. Finally she said, "How long has it been since you had a haircut? You're starting to look pretty bushy."

"I don't know." I said. She was really inspecting me now. "Well, get a haircut and don't wait too long."

I went to Claude Davis' barber shop the next day. I hated getting haircuts, but I liked Claude and he always seemed glad to see me, too. As I was climbing up in his barber's chair he said, "I haven't seen you in so long, I thought maybe you had decided to hair over, but I guess you came to your senses.

Do you want a donut haircut like mine, with a hole in the middle?" He had a bald spot in the back. I told him that I didn't - that I'd just take the regular. "But please don't scalp me this time, I said. Like you usually do." We both laughed. We always kidded like this while he was cutting my hair.

While I was there, several miners came in to take a shower. There were a few places in town where you could take a bath for twenty-five cents. Usually it was in the back of the barber shop.

A lot of miners did that to wash off as much of the coal dust as they could before they went home. Most of the time though, it took more than one bath to get it all off. So, they'd take a bath there and then take another one when they got home. Some of them would take a side trip on the way home and jump in the river and wash off before they went home. But no matter how much they bathed, there was one way you could always tell that a man was a coal miner.

There was a little black line, on the flat part of both eye lids, just where the eye lids meet, that always stayed black. It was almost as though the coal dust went into the pores there, almost like a tattoo and couldn't be washed off.

Seeing the miners going in and out reminded me of something that had happened to me a few months before. I had watched the coal miners all my life and they had always awed me with their stoic endurance and the fact that they had the courage to go down into those black holes every day. They risked death or serious injury every time they went to work.

Once, I had to go to the hospital for an x-ray because I fell out of a tree and when I hit the ground, I landed on a big round rock and really hurt my ribs. I didn't want to go, but Mom said we needed to know if I had any cracked ribs. I went into the emergency room and sat down beside a coal miner who was already there. I could see that his pant leg was torn open on the top of his right thigh and there was a clump of something about the size of a large egg that seemed to be coming out of the skin on his leg. He was just sitting there, saying nothing. I was really curious about what that was on his leg.

It looked wet with blood and it seemed to be jerking slightly and quivering a little. After a while, I just couldn't resist asking him about it. "Excuse me. What happened to your leg?"

13.

He just looked straight ahead for what seemed like a long time. Then he looked over at me and smiled, but you could see in his eyes that he was in deep pain. "A big piece of slate fell on my leg. It ain't broke, 'cause I can still walk a little.....but I reckon it squeezed it so hard it forced some of the muscle to....pop up through the skin." he said quietly.

I couldn't believe that he was sitting there enduring what must have been awful pain and saying nothing. He was just waiting his turn, while other people were being treated for much more trivial things.

"How long have you been sitting here?" I asked. "I told 'em when I come in that I hurt my leg, but they ain't had a chance to look at it yet. I reckon hit's been 'bout an hour and a half since then." he replied. "Did they give you anything for the pain?" I asked. "They ain't yet, but they will directly, I guess." he said.

14.

I must have gone pale listening to what he was saying. I felt silly for even being there with my sore ribs.

I could see a nurse off down the hall. I got up and went down there as fast as I could . "Nurse….there's a man down here who really needs help." I said. "He'll be seen in a few minutes." she said sternly.

"No, he really needs some help now." I pleaded. She looked at me with something like contempt. "Please, can't you just take a look at him? He's in a lot of pain and he's not going to say anything." I said.

She finally decided to do it, because she could see that I wasn't going to stop bugging her. She rigidly and reluctantly walked down the hall to where he was sitting.

When she saw his leg, her face said it all. "My God, why didn't you tell me that was like that? When you walked in, I couldn't see

15.

it because your pant leg was flapped over it." He just smiled and said, "I know'd you'd fix it when you could." That was the kind of man that most of them were and that was the way they lived their lives.

Even in my young life, I had already known three men who had been killed in cave-ins and many more who had black lung disease. It came with the territory that this would happen every now and then and sometimes in clusters. Everybody knew it, but always hoped it wouldn't happen to them or anybody they cared about.

It bothered me to think about the men working in what they called "low coal" with the little Shetland ponies that they used in those days to pull the coal shuttles in and out of the shafts. The little ponies were small enough to work in the "low coal". They also died by the hundreds from the cold and the wet and the coal dust in their lungs.

Most people think of miners as working standing up in little hallway size tunnels. It was really nothing like that, at least not the way most of it was done there, at that time. They worked very often in "low coal", digging out and crawling into tiny passageways which were sometimes smaller than three or four feet high. To make the passages taller meant months more work, blasting and digging, for the same amount of coal.

The hills were peppered with petered out mine shafts where men had worked and sweated and died to get the coal out of the ground. Some of the mines were owned and operated by the big companies.

Others were small "scab" operations run by a few men who could scrape together a little cash. These smaller independent companies would buy a small piece of hillside that they thought might have a little coal hiding underneath. Then they would try to mine it as quickly and cheaply as possible. Sometimes a vein of coal would run between two thick layers of solid granite or other hard rock.

To blast through all that rock was a very expensive and time consuming process, so the shaft would only be dug as big as it had to be.

That meant the coal was often at or below knee level. Many times they worked on their knees and sometimes lying down in mud or water, until the vein was mined out at that point. Then they moved on. It took a certain kind of man to do this job. Besides the obvious danger of cave-ins, there was always the possibility of an explosion from the gases emitted by the coal. Most of these gases have no odor, so they can build up quickly without the men being aware of it.

In those days, they took a small bird with them, in a cage. If there was gas in the shaft, it would kill the bird before the men were effected by it and they would know they had to get out because the gas level was too high. Even the flame from the carbide lights on their helmets could ignite it and cause an explosion.

The job usually burned out the men pretty quickly and most of them were old and broken long before they should have been. There were a few who should never have been in the mines to begin with. One of these was a boy I remember who, "wasn't quite right in the head", as they put it.

Once, he was chopping wood in his yard and a man passing by saw him and said jokingly, "Better be careful, you'll chop off your finger." He stopped chopping wood and said, "I'll chop off my finger, if you will." The man laughed and said, "O.K., go ahead."

He watched in horror as the boy put one of his fingers on the chopping block and chopped it off. Then he handed the man the axe and said, "Your turn". The man ran.

The same boy got a job in the coal mines a few years later, when he was old enough. For reasons no one ever knew, while he was working one day, he decided to chop down one of the main timbers

19.

that supported the shaft where he was working. The other men tried to stop him, but he would not be stopped. They got out as fast as they could and he kept chopping until the shaft caved in and killed him.

There was an old abandoned mine a couple of miles from where I lived. I had been there before, but I had never had the guts to go inside more than a few feet. I always stayed in sight of the sunlight.

One day I went over there with a flashlight, determined to go in far enough to see what it was really like in there. This old mine was really "low coal" and after I got in about twenty or thirty feet, I had to crawl on my hands and knees. I kept the flashlight in my hip pocket until I was far enough in for it to be totally dark. By this time, I was crawling in about six inches of very cold water and there was more water dripping down from the ceiling.

20.

After a few more feet, I could feel my back scraping the ceiling every now and then, so I stopped. I sat there for awhile and looked at the rotting upright and horizontal logs or "timbers" as the miners called them. The "timbers" held up the tons of mountain above.

These "timbers" didn't look as though they could hold it up much longer. I wanted to try to get some idea of what the miners felt like being down there. I knew I couldn't, but I wanted to try. I was starting to get a severe case of claustrophobia.

I tried to hold back the feeling, but my breathing was really beginning to speed up. Trying to imagine working in these conditions didn't seem possible. There was barely enough room to even move and just being in that hole was bad enough.

Finally, I had to get out. I was crawling as fast as I could and I was getting a little panicky. My breathing was even faster now. My heart was pounding and I was in a cold sweat.

When the daylight finally came into view, I thought I'd never get there. After I got out, I sat there for a long time until my breathing got back to something like normal.

One thing I knew for sure. I never wanted to go back into a coal mine again.

I guess I had been dozing or daydreaming and remembering this while Claude was cutting my hair. I sort of came out of my daze when I smelled the tonic he was splashing on me and rubbing into my hair. "Don't put so much of that stuff on me this time." I said. "It makes me smell funny." "Are you sure?" he said. "The girls love you when they smell this." "I guess you won't be needing a shave." "Not quite yet." I said. "What were you thinking about while I was cutting your hair?" he asked. "You looked a little worried." "Oh nothing. I said. "Just coal."

Like most towns in the coal fields, this one was fairly stark and basic, but I never thought of it as a rough town, at least not then. It was just the only town I knew at that point in my life. There was a lot of poverty, but there was also a lot of beauty, in subtle ways, that most people who didn't live there probably wouldn't have noticed. People reached out to help each other when times were hard. In most ways, it was a friendly little town. But, at times, there was also incredible cruelty.

I could always find fun things to do with my dogs or by poking around out in the woods discovering new things to see and do, but there weren't many "fancy" ways to have fun. But there was one thing we had. We had movies - lots of movies.

There were three movie theatres in town - the Lynwood, the Morgan and the Alamo, a lot for a town as small as that and since there weren't many other forms of recreation around there, they all did pretty good business. They always had a double feature and you could stay all day if you wanted to, for the price of one ticket. In those days a ticket cost somewhere between a dime and a quarter. Popcorn was a dime and a Coke cost a nickle.

Sometimes, on Saturdays, I'd make the rounds of all the theatres and see all the movies, sometimes twice. Of course, they also always had the latest episode of a weekly serial and a cartoon, as well as the "Movietone News" or one of the other news reels.

The popcorn bags were about twice as big at the Lynwood theatre as they were at the Morgan, for the same amount of money. So, sometimes after I had seen the movies at the Lynwood, I would buy another bag of popcorn to take with me to the Morgan. When they saw me coming in the door at the Morgan with a bag that said Lynwood theatre on it, they didn't seem to like it. "Don't be bringin' that Lynwood popcorn in here Ronnie." the man said. "You ought to make your bags bigger." I answered over my shoulder, as I went on in.

24.

One of my dogs would often follow me to the movies and when I saw him, I'd turn around and take him home and then go back to the theatre. Occasionally, he'd stay out of sight until I was inside. Then he would wait for a chance to run in, before the door closed, after somebody else went in and later I would feel him sitting down in the floor at my feet.

Sometimes he would stay for the whole movie, but usually Raymond Iron, who was the manager, would see him running through the lobby and a few minutes later he would come in and tap me on the shoulder. "Now Ronnie, I've told you about bringin' that dog in here." I would always say something like, "Raymond, I didn't bring him, he came on his own." "I don't care how he got in here Ronnie, you can't have your dog in the theatre." So, I'd reluctantly take him home and come back later.

Among other things, they showed a lot of B westerns. These movies were usually pretty bad, but there was something basic about them that I liked. As an added attraction, several times a

year, they would have what they called stage shows. These shows

would usually feature one of the B movie cowboys like Tex Ritter,

Tim Holt, Lash Larue or Charles Starrett as the "Durango Kid" and

there were many others. Sometimes they had their sidekick with

them, like Smiley Burnett or Dub Taylor, for comic relief.

The actors would tour small towns all over the country and put on

these live shows between showings of their movies. They would

talk to the kids and do the fast draw and fancy pistol twirling, sing

with a country and western band or do whatever their specialty

was.

The kids all loved it and I never missed one of those shows when

there was one in town. I wasn't crazy about the music, but I loved

the shows.

On one occasion, after one of these shows, I was standing outside the movie theatre when one of the members of the band that was

playing for the stage show that day stopped near where I was

standing, to light a cigarette, on his way out.

I was only a few feet away from him and I wanted to say

something to him. He was still wearing his spangly, fringed

buckskin outfit from the show. I nervously walked over to him,

trying to think of something to say.

Just as I got to him and was about to speak, I noticed another man

coming toward us, walking fairly fast. The approaching man had a

strange look on his face and a second or two later, when he was

approximately in front of the band member, his hand shot up and

he slashed the face of the man in buckskin, from the top of his

forehead, just below the hairline, all the way down to his chin.

Blood went everywhere, including on me.

For an instant time seemed to freeze, as we all tried to take in what had just happened. The man with the knife looked at what he had done and was terrified and shaking.

In that awful moment he seemed to realize that he had done something far more terrible than he had probably intended to do and that he had changed the other man's life forever. I could see that he had a small knife concealed in his blood soaked hand, with only about an inch of the tip of the blade sticking out between his thumb and index finger.

Then he ran and the man who had just had his face slashed ran after him, all the while trying vainly to hold his face together with one hand. He was leaving a trail of blood with every step he took. After a couple of blocks, he gave up and stopped, because he was losing so much blood he could hardly see and it looked as though he might have lost an eye.

I found out the next day that the knife had just missed his left eye.

His face had a deep cut, all the way to the bone in some places, that was over seven inches long and it was going to leave a very bad scar.

When the police finally caught the man, he said he had to do it because the man he slashed had had a fight in a beer joint with his brother, over a girl. He had knocked his brother down and embarrassed him, so he had to get even. I heard later that he only got six months in jail.

Sometimes, it was a rough town.

A couple of days later, I was sitting on the back porch early in the morning watching a red-tailed hawk making lazy circles in the sky while I was waiting for the trucks to bring the convicts to work.

After they showed up, I watched and waited for half an hour or so before I finally got my chance to get past the guards and talk to one of the convicts. I climbed up the creek bank that morning and the guard at that point had been distracted by a small problem further down the road and was looking the other way. One of the convicts was working a few feet away. He saw me walking toward him and gave me a side glance. He didn't seem to be a trustee, but he wasn't in chains either.

"Sure is a hot day ain't it?" I said nervously. He shot me another glance and nodded. He just kept shoveling the small rocks into a wheelbarrow. "You're not a trustee, are you?" I tried again.

"Nope, not yet." he said after a long pause. Then he pointed up the hill at another man. "He is." he said. While I was looking up the hill, he laid down his shovel and started lifting the handles of the wheelbarrow.

"His name's July Culler." he said, as he left pushing his load of rubble down the hill to dump it. "July". I thought. "That's a funny name." I looked to see if the guard had noticed me yet. He hadn't.

Walking on up the hill, my shoes were sinking a couple of inches into the deep powdery dust. You didn't really walk in it, you just sort of waded through it. After a few steps, it was hard to tell where your shoes ended and the ground began.

As I got closer to the other man, he looked at me and smiled. In that smile there was an open friendliness that immediately put you at ease. He was a big man with a strong face, but he was slightly bent from all the years of hard work. He wore the khaki shirt and pants that all the convicts wore, but instead of the cap that all the others wore, he wore a beat up old Stetson hat, with a deep sweat line around it and a heavy layer of dust.

"You Mister Culler?" I asked. "Just call me July." he said. I stuck out my hand. He looked down at me for a second and then extended his huge rough hand. "What's your name?" he asked as we shook hands. "Ronnie." I said. "I live over there, across the creek. I've seen you working over here."

"Well, we do plenty of that." he said. As we talked, he kept

working on a trail of small wires he was stringing up the side of the

hill.

The mountains in that part of the Appalachians are high and very

rugged - one of the oldest mountain ranges on earth. The ground is

rocky and packed hard from millions of years of settling. So

altering the terrain did not come easy and it took a lot of planning.

As he strung the wire, he would stop occasionally and study the

mountain. Then he would make some notations with a little stub

of a pencil on a piece of wrinkled paper he kept in his shirt pocket.

"You drawing a map of the mountain?" I asked. He chuckled at

that. "Well, sort of, I guess," he said, showing me the piece of

paper.

He had drawn a rough sketch of that section of the mountain.

"You see these little circles here? Well, that's where we'll place

the charges." "Charges?" I said. "Yeah, dynamite," he said with a grin. He could see that I really liked the sound of that.

"Dynamite!!" I said. "You gonna blow up the mountain?" He laughed. "Just part of it." he replied. "We'll just blast out enough to loosen up the big rock so we can move it outta here." "Man, I'd love to see that." I said, hardly able to contain myself. "You will." he said with a smile. "But right now, you better scoot, that guard's been giving us the bad eye."

I looked down the hill and saw the guard starting to walk toward us. "O.K., I'm going." I said. "But when you gonna do that blastin'?" "Sometime tomorrow morning." he half whispered. "Now go, before that guard gets here." I ran down the hill, across the dirt road and slid down the creek bank. As I was skipping across on the mossy stones, I could hear the guard yelling, "Damn you boy."

I hardly slept at all that night, thinking about the blasting they were

going to do the next day and I was going to get to see it. As soon
as I was up the next morning, I ran to the kitchen window to see
what was going on across the creek. The men were already there,
but it looked as though they hadn't been there long, because they
were still unloading some of their equipment. I thought about
running across the street to see if my friends, Jerry and Bob
were up so that they could see it too, but I was afraid if I did, I
might miss it myself.

So, I gulped down a glass of orange juice and smeared some
peanut butter on a piece of bread to take with me. After I was out
the door, I could hear the old screen door flapping and my mother
saying, "Where are you going? Don't you want some breakfast?"
"No Ma," I yelled over my shoulder. "I'll be back later."

I knew I couldn't get too close, but I wanted to be sure I didn't miss
anything. I could see July Culler and a few other men stringing
more of that wire. Some of the other men were dragging huge rope

nets up the hill. They must have really been heavy because it took about 10 or 15 men just to drag each one into place.

After all the charges were set and the nets were in place, I heard one of the men call, "Get clear." Everybody moved off the hill pretty fast and I heard somebody call, "All clear?" Then another man answered, "All clear." I was still standing on the opposite creek bank, waiting. Everything got very quiet and it seemed as though they were never going to blow the charges. I could hear my heart pounding hard. Suddenly, I heard a low dull thud and then another one. The side of the hill with the big nets on it just sort of shifted and raised slightly, and then went still again, except for some clouds of dust. I waited a few minutes to see what else was going to happen. Nothing did.

"That's it?" I thought. "That's it?" I was expecting something resembling the blast at "Krakatoa", or at least a few flying boulders. I figured surely they must have done something wrong.

35.

I'd seen a lot of blasts better than this one in the movie serials on Saturdays. I was anxious to talk to July Culler again and find out what went wrong.

The heat was intense. Each day a little hotter and dryer and a little dustier than the last. The creek finally dried up totally, except for a little mud. Now it was easy to get across, except you had to watch out for snakes.

On the really hot days, it was so bright it was almost blinding. You had to squint or shade your eyes almost constantly. No matter what the weather was like, the convicts worked. Occasionally, one of them would drop from the heat and the strain and would have to be carried to a shady place, where they would usually throw a bucket of water in his face and wait until he came around. But most of them stood it pretty well.

There was also an unmistakable sound that the chain gang made.

All the constant hammering and pounding and shoveling and the straining and cursing and groaning, seemed almost as though it had a life of it's own that didn't exist anywhere else.

Sometimes they would sing while they worked and it all seemed to fit. When it stopped, you missed it. I had never heard anything like it. In it you could hear the pain of every mother's son who had ever had to endure this, or something like it - whether he deserved it or not. I'll never forget that lonesome sound.

I remember watching one man, who was chained at the ankles, working with a twelve pound hammer. He would raise the hammer slowly and deliberately until it was at shoulder level, then he would stop for a few seconds and look off into the distance, almost as though he was in a trance, then he would raise the sledge a little higher and let it fall. After it fell, he would again get that far away look in his eye. Then he would slowly start his small ritual all over again.

37.

When I got a chance, I asked July what he thought the man was thinking about. His answer chilled me. "His name's "Big Jake" and he's goin' to be doin' that for the rest of his life. He ain't never goin' to get out, so I reckon he's just trying to imagine he ain't here. He's doin' life." In those days, in that place, doing life really meant the rest of his life, especially for a black man.

I had been wondering what July Culler was in prison for and how long his sentence was. I knew he had been in prison for a long time. I didn't know how much longer he had to go on his sentence and I didn't have the nerve to ask him -- yet.

Every now and then, if they asked permission, the prisoners were allowed to talk to visitors if they had any. Of course, July Culler was about the only one who ever had a visitor and it was always me.

On these occasions, with permission, we could talk for short periods, sometimes during their lunch break, if the guards were in a good mood - but they always kept a close eye on us. It was during one of these short conversations that he asked me what seemed like a strange request.

"Ronnie, I wonder if you could git me some old toothbrushes?" I looked at him for a second and sort of half laughed. "Old toothbrushes? What do you want with old toothbrushes?" He just smiled. "If you need a toothbrush, I'll get you one," I said. He laughed and said, "Naw, I don't want 'em for brushin' my teeth. I got one for that. I got somethin' else I use 'em for. Somethin' like you ain't never seen."

This really had me curious. "Like what." I asked. "What else can you do with them?" "You'll see. I'll show you tomorrow at lunch time, if I can."

Just see if you can find me a few," he said, as he went back up the hill to work. All the way home, I kept wondering what else you could do with old toothbrushes and where I was going to find any. I could remember seeing my Dad, when he still lived at our house, using a toothbrush to put polish on his shoes, but I'd never done it myself. I wasn't much on shining my shoes.

The more I thought about it, I seemed to remember that that old shoe box my Dad had used for his shoe shining stuff was still in the back of the closet. As soon as I got home, I checked and there it was and when I dug through the junk in it, I found three toothbrushes, one for black polish and one each for brown and cordovan polish. I didn't know if July would want them with shoe polish on them though. I took them anyway. I decided that I'd take him my own toothbrush too and my mother's, if I could.

The next morning after I had brushed my teeth, I asked my mother about it. "Ma, don't you think we need some new toothbrushes? These are all chewed up."

She looked at me and said, "Toothbrushes?" "What are you talking about? What's wrong with the toothbrushes?" She had that look on her face, like she knew I was up to something. "It's just that they're all chewed up, Ma. I could go down to the store and get us a couple of new ones." She still had that look on her face.

Then, she decided I must be on the level because she couldn't figure out what kind of trouble I could be planning with toothbrushes. Finally, she said, "O.K., but be sure you get two just like the ones we've got. I like those." I was already halfway out the door. I ran the two blocks to the store, got the toothbrushes and told Mr. Carver to put them on our bill. I was allowed to charge things, as long as they weren't too frivolous, like candy.

As I went out the back door of the store, I noticed a woman sitting on a bag of feed, nursing her baby. She had her breast totally exposed and I just stood there and stared at her for a long time.

41.

There was a cigarette hanging out of her mouth and she didn't seem to mind or even notice that I was standing there, ten feet away, staring at her. She was a little ragged, but she looked beautiful to me. She was, maybe, fifteen years old and the baby she was nursing was her second child. The other one was playing in the dirt in front of her.

Finally, her husband came out of the store. The carbide light on his miner's helmet was still lit and he was covered with coal dust from the night shift he had just worked. He looked at me and said, "How you doin', boy?" I just stood there and watched them leave. I thought about the girl all the way home.

So now, I had five toothbrushes for July. It made me feel good to know I had something to give him, that he seemed to want, even if it was just a few old toothbrushes.

I stood on the creek bank and watched the men work for awhile.

42.

It was still pretty early in the morning and I was having a hard time waiting until noon to give July the toothbrushes. Besides, then he was going to tell me what he did with them. I thought about trying to slip by the guard and give them to him right then, but I figured I'd better wait until noon. If one of the guards saw me give him something while he was working, it might get him in trouble.

Most of the guards just did the job for the money and some were a little afraid, though they tried not to show it. But there was one guard who was different. There was a quiet meanness about him. He didn't say much, but he could burn a hole through you with a look. His name was R.D. Turner and everybody knew that sooner or later he would probably kill somebody. The convicts all feared him and hated him and that was just the way he liked it. He had found the job of his dreams. He could be a bully and get paid for it.

The first thing you noticed about him was his redness. His hair was red and his face was so red he looked as though he had been holding his breath. Of course, his nickname was "Red", but the convicts had another name for him. They called him "Red Dog", though never to his face.

Why he tolerated me coming around, I'll never know. Maybe he thought my being there would cause trouble and he was always hoping for that. I overheard a conversation he was having with one of the other guards one day. The guard was saying he hoped they didn't have any trouble. Turner laughed and said, "Trouble? I love trouble. I thrive on it." The other guard was just as scared by that as I was.

On days when he was working there was a nervous tension in the air and he would often taunt some of the convicts by just staring at them, hoping to get some kind of reaction. If he got the reaction he wanted, even a slight look of contempt, he would have a couple of

the guards take the convict to what he called "the classroom" - a
little one car garage that was left after a house had been torn down
to make room for the new road - where he would, "teach him a
lesson." When a convict came back from one of these sessions, he
was usually in pretty bad shape, sometimes missing a few teeth.

Most of the men got along with most of the guards, at least as well
as could be expected, but more and more the convicts were
beginning to see Turner's attitude as a challenge. Even the other
guards were uneasy about this, but there was nothing they could
say or do. He was in charge. He seemed to think this was a good
way to maintain discipline. Actually, it made things much worse
and more explosive a lot of the time.

All the other guards carried twelve gauge shotguns, but Turner
carried a lever action 30/30 Winchester rifle. Every now and then
he would take a pot shot at a rat, if he saw one on the creek bank.
One shot would usually take the rat's head off. He was a very

good shot and he wanted all the convicts to see that. The crack of
that rifle, whenever he did this, raised the hair on everybody's
neck. The convicts all understood.

July told me that Turner shot a man a few years back. The man
lived, but he never walked again. Not long after that, Turner got
promoted to head guard. He had a reputation from many years and
many other chain gangs. He wore it like a badge of honor and he
loved living up to that reputation.

I stood there for awhile, watching Turner. He saw me looking at
him and seemed to take it as a compliment. It wasn't meant that
way.

I remember thinking that it was hard to imagine the sheer terror of
being under the control of a man like him. He was far more of a
criminal than most of the men he was "guarding".

It seemed like forever, but noon finally rolled around and when it did, I was there waiting for the men to take their break. I saw July coming down the hill and he gave me a big grin when he saw me.

"Hi, Ronnie, how are ya, boy? Let me git somethin' to eat and we'll talk." He went to the mess truck, got a plate full and on the way back, he stopped and asked one of the guards if he could talk to me for a few minutes. Then he came back to the old fence where I was sitting.

"Were you able to git me any toothbrushes?" he asked as he sat down on the fence. "I got you five," I said, "but three of 'em have got shoe polish on 'em." "That don't matter at all." he said. "Let me see 'em." I pulled them out of my hip pocket and gave them to him. When he saw them, he lit up. "Say, these are real nice ones. Two green ones, a blue one, a red and a yellow one. These'll do just fine. Thank you, Ronnie. I got somethin' for you too. I'll git it, soon's I finish eatin'."

"What was it you were gonna show me?" I asked. "You'll see, soon as I git done eatin'." he said. He ate that plate full and then went back for seconds. I thought he'd never finish eating his lunch.

When he did, he said, "I'll be back in a minute." He took the empty plate back to the mess truck and then said to the guard, "I need to git my rings out of the other truck." The guard nodded that it was O.K.

He came back in a few minutes with an incredibly wrinkled old brown paper bag that was bulging from whatever was in it. "I'll bet you ain't never seen nothin' like these, Ronnie." he said, as he opened the bag and poured out some of the contents into his hand. They were rings, brightly colored rings. Each ring was four or five different colors. They were really beautiful and extremely well made. "Where did you get these?" I asked. "I made 'em." he said through a big smile.

"This is what I do with the toothbrushes. Here, take a few and look at 'em." I took three or four rings and looked at them carefully. The colors really sparkled in the sunlight. "You make these out of toothbrushes?" I asked, in disbelief. "That's right." he said.

Each ring was made out of several different colored pieces of plastic that had evidently been melted and shaped to make the different designs. They showed no evidence of ever having been part of a toothbrush. It looked as though he had melted the plastic totally and remolded it in the general shape he wanted. Then, I guess, he would sand it and carve it and polish it, so that it would fit together with the other parts of the ring, like finely inlaid wood.

Some had initials inlaid on the sides, some had intricate designs running through them. Every ring was different and he must have had two hundred rings in the bag. "How do you make 'em?" I asked.

"That's a long story, son. It takes me five or ten days workin' in my spare time, which ain't much, to make each one. It's pretty complicated." I couldn't get over how intricate they were and how different they all were. "They're really beautiful July." I said. "Thank you, Ronnie. Listen, I ain't got no money to give you, so why don't you take a couple of them rings for yourself."

"What for, July? You don't owe me anything for those old toothbrushes." He smiled. "These toothbrushes ain't the first things you brought me, boy," he said.

"You been bringin' me apples and ice water and other stuff right along." He hesitated for a second. "I appreciate it. So, now I can give you a little somethin' too. Go ahead, pick a couple you like."

I shyly picked through the rings and finally pulled out two that I liked. They were a little big for my fingers, but I liked the way they looked. "Thank you, July, I really like 'em." He could see that they were too big. "You'll grow into 'em. I'm glad you like like 'em." he said.

We both just sat there looking at the ground for awhile without saying anything. July folded down the top of the bag with the rings in it. Finally, I said, "July, can I ask you a question?" He nodded that it was O.K. I nervously continued, "Well, I was just wonderin'.....what they put you in prison for."

He didn't say anything for awhile. I was afraid I had gone too far. Then he said slowly, "Ronnie, I took somethin' that wasn't mine. I didn't have nothin' and my family didn't have nothin' and I couldn't git no job. So, I stole some money. I never had done nothin' like that or been in no trouble before, but I was feelin' pretty desperate and I did something I know'd was wrong. I shouldn't have, but I did and now I'm payin' the price."

"I stole fifty dollars and they gave me ten years. I've served nine

51.

years, six months and four days of it. Seven of them years I was in chains, bustin' rocks, before they made me a trustee.

My daddy was a slave. I was born when he was pretty close to sixty. He was born 'bout 1850. We never know'd for sure when he was born, since they never kept no records on slaves. In them days they'd usually just put the names of new babies and the date when they was born, in their bibles. If they put his in there, I guess it must'a got lost somewhere along the way. Mr. Lincoln set 'em free when my daddy was 'round fifteen. He died in 1934 when he was....'bout eighty four, I guess.

He always told me never to get in no trouble. Then I was dumb enough to go out and bring all this misery on myself. He used to tell me stories about what it was like bein' a slave. He used to say it was as close to hell as you could git and still be walkin' around alive. It must'a been a lot like this. I reckon it sure couldn't have been much worse."

I was amazed at what July was telling me. It was like something out of a history book. I wanted to say something, but I didn't know what to say, so I just kept quiet and listened and learned.

It didn't seem possible that his father could have been a slave. But, when you thought about it and added it all up, the years seemed to fit. It all made sense and it logically followed that many of these men were probably the sons or, at least, grandsons of slaves. From what I had heard about it, I had always thought of the Civil War as being a long, long time ago. I guess at that time, it really hadn't been all that long since it ended and it was still casting a very long shadow.

"Nine years and six months," I thought. That meant he had been in jail almost as long as I had been alive. It seemed impossible to me. "I hope you didn't mind me askin'," I said. "That's all right son, I know'd you was wonderin' and I would probably have told you sooner or later anyway."

53.

After a long pause, he said slowly, "Ronnie, let me tell you somethin' son. There's a lot you can learn from this, 'bout what not to do in your own life. Don't never do nothin' that'll give 'em a chance to put you in a place like this." "I won't," I said. "Ever think about just walking away, July? You're a trustee, you could."

"Sure, I've thought about it" he said, "but how far do you think I'd get. You think old "Red Dog" over there ain't just itchin' to shoot me?"

"Even if he didn't shoot me, bad things can happen when there's nobody around to see. I learned a long time ago that I was goin' to have to be careful around him or I'd never make it outta here. Besides, I don't exactly blend in with the locals, ya know. I'd be stupid to mess up now. I've almost done it."

I could hear the guards calling the men back to work. "Well, Ronnie, I got to go. Thanks again for the toothbrushes." He got up to go, then seemed to remember something. "Oh, I almost

forgot." he said. "There was one other little thing I meant to give

you."

"With all this diggin' we do around here, every now and then we

dig up one of these." He was pulling something out of his shirt

pocket while he was telling me this.

"It was left here by some people who used to live here, a long time

ago. I thought you might want it." He handed me a perfect black

flint arrowhead. I was amazed. This was like magic to me. "Wow

July, I love Indian things. This is really a nice one. Thank you....

for all this...the rings and the arrowhead. I really like 'em a lot."

He grinned. "Well, then we both had a pretty good day. I got my

toothbrushes and you got some stuff you like too."

"Pretty good, huh?" We both laughed. "Oh one more thing,

Ronnie. Would you do me one more favor?" "Sure." I said.

He looked around to see if anybody could hear him and then he said, almost in a whisper, "I wonder if you could get me a knife?"

"A knife?" I thought. I couldn't believe he was actually asking me for a knife. It took me a few seconds to be able to look him straight in the eye and he could see that it bothered me. "A knife, July?" I said slowly. "Now don't git the wrong idea, Ronnie," he said. "I don't want it for no bad reason."

"Then why do you want it, July?" I asked. "I just need a little knife to use when I make my rings," he said "and you can't tell nobody about it. Not even your friends, cause they might tell the guards." He looked around and the guard was motioning for him to get back to work.

"You think about it, Ronnie, but please don't tell nobody." As he turned to go, he looked at me with a questioning look, to see if I would keep his secret. "I won't tell anybody, July." I said. "Thank

56.

you, son," he said with relief. Then he turned and waved as he walked back up the hill. I stood there for a few minutes thinking about what he had asked me.

I didn't know what to do and I couldn't even ask anybody.

It was almost time for school to start and that was going to change things considerably for the road gang. Suddenly there would be hundreds of kids, from six to eighteen, coming and going and gawking at the prisoners from a distance. Security on the prisoners got a lot tighter.

It wasn't so bad for July, because he was a trustee, but they all knew they had to be very careful or these kids could cause a lot of trouble for them. The fact that school was about to start again didn't make me very happy either. Sitting in a classroom all day wasn't exactly my idea of fun.

When the first day of school finally did come, one of the first things they did was call us all to the auditorium for a little lecture and a warning about the prisoners and how dangerous they were.

While we were listening to this, I couldn't help smiling. They were telling all the kids how dangerous the convicts were and I had been over there talking to July for months now.

There was no doubt that there were some bad men and some who were very dangerous on that road gang, but there were a few who should never have been there. July was at the top of that list.

For these men, the major crime was being born in a time and place where the very essence of their being was perceived to be a bad or even evil thing, because they were different. All the history that had preceded their birth in this place had left them struggling from the first day.

Any chain gang was bad enough, but a black chain gang in the segregated south was hell on earth, because it was assumed that they had it coming, just because of who they were. Their pain didn't matter, because they weren't even considered to be really human. Any punishment they received, no matter how cruel or unwarranted, was thought to be justified.

Then I remembered again that July had asked me for a knife. July was a good man. I knew he was. No one could ever convince me that he would ever hurt anybody. Still, if I gave him a knife, it could get him in trouble and maybe even keep him from getting out when he was supposed to. I really didn't know what to do.

I showed all my friends the rings July had given me. They were all very impressed. "You got 'em from one of the convicts?" they asked, as though they thought I was making it up. "Where did he get 'em?" " He made 'em." I said with pride, "Out of old toothbrushes."

They all examined the rings very carefully.

"Toothbrushes?" they asked. "How could he make these out of toothbrushes? They don't look nothin' like toothbrushes." "Besides that," one boy said, "them convicts are all niggers. They ain't smart enough to make anything like this."

That really made me mad. "They're a hell of a lot smarter than you are," I said. "July Culler made these rings from nothin' but old toothbrushes and he had almost nothin' to work with." After I said that, I realized that July probably did really need the knife. I suppose it was then that I decided to get it for him.

That Sunday, my mother and I were invited to my Uncle Bill and Aunt Naomi's house for dinner. I really loved Bill and Naomi. Bill was almost like a father to me. They were both always good to me and Aunt Naomi was a great cook. I can still taste those big fluffy biscuits she used to make. They must have been two inches thick and four inches across. They smelled heavenly and they were mouth wateringly good, like everything she made.

During dinner, we talked about a lot of things - the weather, the convicts, school, Uncle Bill's lumber business and Naomi's great cooking. I kept thinking about how in the world I could sneak July a knife without getting caught. They all noticed that I was distracted. "What are you thinking about, Ronnie?" Uncle Bill asked. "Oh, nothin'." I said. "Just school."

After dinner, we were sitting out on the porch talking as it was getting dark. Uncle Bill brought an apple out with him. He pulled out his pocket knife to cut it with. Then he polished the apple on his sleeve a little and looked it over before slicing it. There was a little dark spot on the side of the apple, so he stuck the knife straight in on all four sides of the dark spot and pulled out a little square piece of apple, sort of like plugging a watermelon. As I watched him do this, I was beginning to figure out how I was going to get the knife to July.

At school the next day, I was still thinking about it. Boone, the boy who sat next to me, didn't have a pencil that day, so I broke mine into two pieces and gave him half of it.

The teacher saw me do that and was very annoyed. She walked over to me and asked me to hold out my hand. When I did, she gave me about four good whacks with a ruler across the palm.

"What was that for?" I asked, through what must have been a fairly pained and surprised expression. "That's for breaking your pencil." she said. "But Boone didn't have one." I stammered. "No excuses." she said quickly.

A few days after that, someone came to the classroom door and asked for Boone. He didn't come back that day. I found out later that Boone's father had died.

The fact that his father had died was horrible enough, but the circumstances of his death made the situation even more strange and ethereal. He had been nipped by a dog, but thought nothing of it at the time. He didn't find out until it was too late that the dog had rabies. It was a terrible and very frightening thing even to think about and I really felt sad for Boone and his family. The whole town was affected by it. I know I had nightmares about it for months after that.

The road was really coming along now. It was already beyond the school and the convicts were working on the first big curve. No matter which way they went, it didn't get any easier. Another thing that had wiped out the road they were replacing was the heavy rain and flooding that came every few years. When there was heavy rain, there was no place for the water to go except through the floor of the valley. Sometimes whole sections of road would just disappear. For that matter, just about everything around there, at one time or another, had been flooded or badly damaged by the floods.

In some cases, whole houses had been washed away in one piece. So, they were trying to reinforce the road to make it a lot more durable than the one that had been there. They were building walls to try and channel the water, but everybody knew it was a lost cause in the long run, because when it got really bad, the water was so fast and so deep it always overcame all the efforts to stop it.

On the first straight section of road, they had had to blast out the side of a mountain and now on the first curve, they would have to divert the flow of the creek. In the meantime, everybody was still using the old road, which was across the creek from the one that was being rebuilt. The old road was a very narrow, one and a half lane, "blacktop".

Work on the road was about to encounter a new problem. They were now approaching an old bridge with an arched steel frame. The bridge was set at a very odd angle to the road and it was up on a knoll, which put it much higher than the road. The entrance up to the bridge from one direction was gradual and easy enough to use, but from the other direction it was very difficult, if not dangerous, to try to get on it.

It had always been a problem and the engineers thought they had figured out how to fix it, according to their plans, but now that they were there working on it, they were having second thoughts about it.

Several times I saw them going over their plans. A couple of times I heard them arguing about it. They seemed to know it wasn't right, but had decided to go ahead as planned, because they just couldn't agree on how to change it. Then, one day when I walked up the road to see July, I found him sitting down, during his lunch break, drawing something on a piece of paper. "What'ya drawing July?" When I looked over his shoulder, I could see that he was sketching the ramp up to the bridge.

65.

"The angle's all wrong. I'm just tryin' to figure out how to make it work better." he said, as he continued to draw. "You see, if we could build up the bank a little more on this side, take out them two trees and that big rock over there and have the road curve around here and sort of fan out, like this, it'd make it a lot easier to get on the bridge from this direction."

"Then maybe we could add a little wall or a rail right here." he said, as he showed me his ideas on the sketch. "So the cars would have to start up the hill at a better angle to the bridge."

"Can they change the way it is?" I thought they had to do it the way it is on their plans over there." I said. July laughed. "Naw, this ain't no super highway we're building here. It's just a little ole country road. They change it all the time, from them plans, dependin' on how the ground has changed or if they think another way of doin' it would make it work better. There ain't nothin' unusual about that.

The only thing that stays pretty much the same is where it starts and where it ends up. Believe me son, I've worked on a whole bunch of these little roads and a few big ones too. A lot more than I want to remember."

I was looking at what he had drawn. "I don't know much about it July, but that looks a lot better to me than what they've been talking about."

"Why don't you tell 'em about it?" I said. He laughed. "I don't think they'd be much interested in what I think about it." He wadded up the piece of paper and threw it in a big steel drum that they used for debris. Then we talked for a few more minutes before he had to get back to work. After he left, to work on the other side of the hill, I waited till he was out of sight, then I reached down in the big can and got the piece of paper. I flattened it out and looked at it again for awhile. It really did seem like a much better idea to me.

I still had a pencil from school in my shirt pocket, so I laid the piece of paper on a rock and printed July Culler on it at the bottom. Then I walked over to the back of the truck where the engineers had their plans laid out. I could see that the men were up on the bridge, measuring and making notations.

They had left their big drawings lying there in the bed of the truck with a few rocks on them to hold them down. I picked up one of the rocks and put July's drawing on top of theirs. Then I put the rock back on top of it, so it wouldn't blow away. I looked around to see if anybody had seen me. They hadn't. They were so used to me by now, they just ignored me most of the time.

I got away from the drawings as soon as I could. Then I walked down the road a short distance and waited to see what happened. After about fifteen minutes, the engineers started back down to the truck where the plans were. I couldn't wait to see what would happen.

When the first man saw the piece of paper, he looked at it for a moment, then he passed it around to the others. Then they were all nodding and discussing it. I wanted to stay, but after a few minutes, I had to get back to school.

I wasn't able to get up there for a few days after that, but when I did, I was surprised and happy to see that they had built the bridge ramp almost exactly the way July had sketched it. I searched around for awhile before I found July and when I did, I must have had a big grin on my face. "They must have liked your idea, July." I said. "They built it just the way you drew it, after they saw your picture." He looked at me as though he thought I was crazy.

"What do you mean, after they saw my picture?" he said.

"I got the picture you drew out of the trash. Then I put your name on it and put it over there on their truck. I saw them looking at it. Didn't they tell you?"

He couldn't believe what he was hearing. He didn't say anything for awhile. "You shouldn't have done that, Ronnie. I know you meant well, but that ain't a safe thing to do. They ain't never goin' to admit that that was my idea and they mighta' come down hard on me, cause they thought I put it there.

Then I felt really rotten. "I'm sorry July. I just thought you had a better idea. I didn't mean to get you in trouble." He just looked at the ground for awhile. "Don't worry about it son. It looks like it worked out O.K." Then he smiled. "You're right, it was a better idea, but don't expect them to give me no credit for it. Just remember, you have to be real careful about stuff like that. It's dangerous. You understand now, don't you?" "It just doesn't seem right July," I said. "They did it the way you drew it."

"Life ain't always fair Ronnie. I'm in prison and that's just the way it is." I just nodded.

70.

It was almost time for some of the berries to be ripe and ready to pick. I knew a place, far up on one of the mountains, where I could get quite a few. There were a couple of walnut trees near there too, so I could also get a few of those while I was up there. Then I could sell them to some of the neighbors, which I sometimes did to pick up a little pocket change.

It was a pretty long, steep climb, up past the old reservoir and much, much higher, past the "Swiss cheese rock", as I called it. I called it that because it was full of holes. It looked as though it had been heavily lapped by water for a very long time, eons ago.

There were places up there where it looked the way it must have looked ten thousand years ago, or more.

In some of the shady places among the trees, the undergrowth was incredibly thick with huge ferns and blankets of lush green moss. It looked almost like a rain forest. I remember standing there looking at it, thinking that this must have been the way it had all looked when the Indians were there.

Besides the berries and the walnuts, there was another reason I wanted to get up there near the top. It was so high up that I knew of a cliff that I thought would give me a fairly good view of the new road, as far as they had built it up to that point.

I took the biggest knapsack I had and some extra bags to hang on it, to hold as many berries and walnuts as I could pick. I started early and by the time I got up there and found the cliff I was looking for, it was almost 10:00 o'clock in the morning.

The view was even better than I had thought it would be. It was almost like being up in a plane looking down at it and the road looked great from up there. It looked almost like a ribbon winding along beside the creek. I wished July could have seen the way it looked from there.

I sat there and looked for quite awhile. It was beautiful. Then, I decided I'd better get busy picking the berries and walnuts. I picked as many as I thought I could carry home. Then I started back.

There were all kinds of stories about some sort of strange animal that lived somewhere up there in the woods, further than most people would ever go.

I had heard the stories about it all my life and no matter who was telling the story, they always described it the same way. They were very afraid of this thing, whatever it was. I realized many years later that what they had described was a "Big Foot" type creature. Though they never had any sort of name for it. To my knowledge, at that time, there had never been any stories in the press about anything like that. The reports of that sort of thing came much later, with the Himalayan "Yeti" and then "Big Foot", in the U.S. and other places.

I was in the woods a lot and I camped out deep in the woods many, many times over the years, but I never saw it or heard it. They said it had a blood curdling yell, too. I was always hoping I would see it, if there was anything to see, but I never did.

So, whenever I went up in the woods, I was usually sort of halfway thinking about that. But, on this particular day, everything had been pretty uneventful.

After climbing back down for awhile, I guess I was about a third of the way down, when I heard some shuffling in the leaves just over a little rise, off to my left and I thought, "maybe this will be the day when I see the thing." So, I very quietly tip toed over a few feet in that direction and looked over the rise to see what it was. I had hoped to see something really unusual, but what I was looking at was nothing like what I had hoped to see and it sent a very cold chill down my spine.

About twenty yards down the hill was a full grown male cougar and he was a big one. He had seen me, too. I couldn't believe what I was seeing and neither could he. He was looking me right in the eye and neither of us moved for a very long moment. I knew he could easily kill me if he thought of me as any kind of threat or if he saw me as prey or if he just felt like it.

I couldn't run, because I knew I'd never make it. Besides, there was nowhere to run to, that he couldn't get me. I couldn't even go up a tree, because he could do that too. I didn't move a muscle.

After what seemed like forever, he narrowed his eyes slightly and looked at me with a look on his face that said, "Don't do anything stupid", as he turned and slowly walked off around the side of the hill. He turned and looked back at me once. Then he was gone. I guess he wasn't hungry.

As soon as he was out of sight, I got out of there fast and got back

down the mountain as quickly as I could, before he changed his
mind and came back.

I told some of my friends about it and they all laughed. They
seemed to think I was making the whole thing up, because nobody
had ever seen a cougar around there. At least, not that they knew
of. Well, somebody had seen one now and it was me.

The next night, about a mile up the river from there, two large dogs
were killed when they heard something out in the chicken coop
and went out to check on it. The man who owned the dogs said
later that from the tracks he found and the marks on the dogs, it
looked as though some kind of big cat might have done it.

I knew who it was.

I still hadn't slipped the knife to July and the more I thought about
it, the more nervous I became. On Sunday afternoon, when the
men weren't working, I rode my bicycle up the old blacktop to the

"Bend of Slate", where the convict camp was. It was about four miles from where I lived. I had heard about the camp, but I had never seen it. It was a fairly long little trip on a bike and on the way up, I saw old Barney Taylor plowing his field with his old horse, "Dan".

The two of them had been together for a long time and they looked as though they belonged together. They both had a lot of strength and dignity in their old age. Barney was close to ninety and I had heard that the horse was around twenty five.

Old "Dan" was the most swaybacked horse anybody had ever seen. He was a horse of normal height at the shoulders and rump, but in the middle, his back looked almost like a big **U**. When Barney rode him into town for supplies, he wasn't really sitting on him as much as he was sitting down <u>in</u> him - down about where the horse's lungs should have been. But, they both seemed to have a lot of spunk. I waved and kept on going.

The camp was right next to Benny Sax's junk yard - acres of rusting relics - some with grass growing inside them. There was one beautiful, but battered, 1939 Lincoln Zephyr with a V-12 engine. At least, that's what it said on the hood. It seemed ancient to me, even though it was only about ten years old then.

Benny Sax was a huge man who weighed well over three hundred pounds and was at least 6' 4" or so. He always wore bib overalls or "overhauls", as they were called there and he was never without his railroad hat. It was one of those hats that looked as though it was made out of an old striped denim mattress cover.

He didn't like having the prison camp so close to his junk yard, but he knew there was nothing he could do about it. He would stand there and mumble and grumble and mutter to himself, "Damn convicts". But, he wanted the new road because he figured it would be good for business and business was something that Benny knew about.

So, it seemed worth it to him to put up with the camp until the work was done.

Benny would sell you just about anything if the price was right. He was fairly well off financially and he usually drove the latest model Cadillac.

I remember once a man came through there who was driving a new Cadillac, exactly like the one Benny had. It was even the same color. The stranger's car had a huge scrape and a deep dent on the driver's side door, from an encounter he had had with a coal truck. The man stopped and asked Benny if he had a door that would fit his car. Benny said no. The man could see Benny's shiny new Cadillac sitting there. So, he asked him if he could buy the door off that car. Benny looked at him as though he thought he was kidding, but after a few seconds thought, he said, "Yep, but it's gonna cost you."

Benny took the door off his Cadillac and sold it to the man. He drove his car around with no door on the driver's side for about two months while he waited for another door, that he ordered, to come from Detroit.

When I finally got to the camp that day, I could only sit across the creek and watch. The camp was just a bunch of tents on wooden platforms and there was a big steel mesh fence with barbed wire on top, around the whole thing. There were guards walking around among the trees.

There seemed to be even more guards here than they had on the road gang and they were all armed with their ever present twelve gauge shot guns.

I couldn't see July, but I could see some of the other prisoners milling around, smoking, talking and playing cards. A few were pitching horseshoes.

It seemed unbelievable to me that this was the extent of their world. That all they did was break their backs on the road gang all day and then come here at night.

Some of them were laughing, though most of them never even smiled. It was hard to see how any of them could ever laugh in this hell they were living in, but sometimes a few of them did. One thing that made things a little more difficult for the convicts, at least in a subtle way, was the fact that there was often a smell in the air that was unmistakable. It was something that reminded most of the men that there were a lot of things they had had to give up while they were in prison.

There were one or two moonshine stills within smelling distance of the men, at the camp where they stayed at night and near the road where they worked during the day. If the wind was just right, you could get a pretty good whiff sometimes.

The smell was really strong because some of the whisky was over 150 proof. When they first smelled it, they looked at each other with that, "Is that what I think it is?" look on their faces. They just couldn't believe it.

They talked about it a lot and found it pretty hard to ignore. They also resented the fact that a lot of them were in jail for doing a lot less than the moonshiners were doing here so blatantly.

Every now and then a moonshiner would get caught, but most of the time they got away with it. It always seemed to me that it would be pretty easy to catch them by just following the smell.

Some of them put their stills deeper in the woods so they wouldn't get caught, but it wasn't unusual to smell it from the road. So, there were a few that weren't far away. This particular day you could really smell it.

I could see a few of the convicts sitting there with their eyes closed taking a few deep breaths. Once, when I saw them doing this during a break from work, I heard July say to one of them, "You can't get drunk on the fumes." The other man said, "Maybe not, but I'm sure tryin'." They both laughed.

I sat there on my bike and watched for awhile. Then it started to rain. It had been so hot and dry for so long, the rain was welcome. I just sat there and let it rain on me for awhile, then I started home. On the way back, I saw Barney and old "Dan" still plowing. They hadn't even slowed down at all. I stopped for a moment and watched them. "Should you be plowin' in the rain, Barney?" I yelled. "Well, we got to git her done." he yelled back. I used to love listening to old Barney talk when he came to town. He was almost like a time capsule from another age. If he was talking about somebody he didn't like, he would say something like, "He ain't worth the ball and powder it would take to blow him to hell."

I think this may have gone back to the days of the cap and ball, muzzle loading rifles from before the Civil War or possibly even further back to the old flintlock rifles from the Revolutionary War, which his grandfather probably fought in.

He told me once that he remembered his father coming back from the Civil War. He said, "Yep, me and my Ma and all my brothers and sisters went up to Abingdon to wait for him. They was a string of walkin' men passin' through there that went on for days. They was all jist tryin' to git home, cause the war was over.

A lot of em' was hurt bad and never did make it home, cause they died along the way. Quite a few didn't have no shoes and some of 'em had walked for hundreds of miles. They was men in that line who wore gray and others that wore blue. Some was brothers who had fought on opposite sides of it.

We was jist one of hundreds of families that was waitin' there,

hopin' to see their daddy or their brother or their son.   In most
cases their people never even know'd whether the man they was
lookin' for was alive or dead.

After waitin' about two days, we finally seen my daddy comin'
and he was all tore up. We was all cryin' and huggin' him. He
was cryin' too. He picked me up, I reckon I was about five or so
and he put his hat on my head. I thought that was really
somethin'."

"What color was his hat?" I asked. Barney smiled and said, "My
daddy's hat was blue."

I sat there in the rain and watched him plow for awhile longer then
I started on home. By the time I got home I was soaked to the
bone, but it felt good.

The next morning on the way out the door, I grabbed one of the big
red apples that Mom had in that bowl on the dining room table.

I already had the two bladed pocket knife that my Dad gave me stuffed in my pocket.

All morning in school, I had this empty feeling in the pit of my stomach, just thinking about slipping July the pocket knife, but if I was going to do it, it would have to be today. Turner took Mondays off. So, it had to be while he wasn't there. I wouldn't have the nerve to do it with him there. At lunch, I went to the john, got in one of the stalls and locked the door.

I sat there looking at the apple for a long time, rolling it over and over in my hands, wondering whether or not I should actually go through with it.

I guess I knew all along I would do it, but I still had to think about it a little bit more. I got out the pocket knife and opened the longest blade. After studying the apple for awhile, I decided that the best place to cut out the plug would be around the indentation where the stem was. I stuck the knife in deep on four sides around the stem and angled it just a little each time, so the plug came to a sharp point.

I was being very careful not to damage the way the stem hole looked on the outside. When I got it loose, I pulled the chunk out. I carefully reamed out the hole on the inside to make it big enough to hold the knife.

It was a lot more difficult than I thought it would be to make the hole bigger on the inside without messing it up on the outside. It looked pretty good though and finally, it was big enough to hold the knife. I cut most of the white part of the plug off and left just enough to rest on the end of the folded up knife after it was inside. The plug was a little shaky, but as long as I held my finger on it, the apple looked normal.

All this took about ten minutes, which left me fifty minutes or so of my lunch hour, to get up the road to where the convicts were working now and give the apple to July. I didn't want to seem too anxious or nervous. The guards might think something was fishy if I seemed uneasy.

On my way out, as I was running across the lawn in front of the school, a boy ran into me and knocked the apple out of my hand. It rolled a few feet on the grass, but miraculously, the whole thing stayed together and the apple still looked the same. I picked it up, had a quick look at it to be sure that it was okay and kept on going.

They were working about a quarter of a mile up the road. When I got within sight of the chain gang, I slowed down to a walk and caught my breath.

I couldn't see July right away, so I went over near the mess truck and looked around. Finally, I saw him sitting on a big rock eating lunch. Wouldn't you know it? There was a guard standing about

ten feet away from him. I didn't know whether I should go ahead
with it now, since the guard was that close, but by that time July
had seen me.

He smiled that big smile and motioned me over. When I got a
little closer, I heard him say to the guard, "You don't mind if I talk
to the boy for a few minutes, do you?" The guard said that it was
okay. As I slowly walked past the guard toward July, I was
squeezing that apple so hard that it was a wonder it didn't split.

"Hi, July," I said nervously. He could see that something was
different about me. "What's the matter, boy? You feeling O.K.?"
he asked. I gave the guard a quick glance to see if he was paying
any attention to any of this. I felt as though I looked like guilt
itself. The guard was just sort of looking past us, lost in thought,
as he pulled out his wrinkled pouch of Red Man chewing tobacco
and put a fresh wad in his cheek. Then he wandered over to the
mess truck. I was relieved that he was at least a little further away.

"What's wrong, Ronnie?" July asked again. "Nothing, July." I said. I gave the guard another quick look. He was talking to the cook. "I've got something for you." I said, holding out the apple. I turned my back on the guard. "Well, thank you, son. That's a real beauty." July said, as he reached out to take the apple. He put his hand on the apple, but I didn't let go of it.

He looked at me for a second with a question on his face. "There's something in the apple." I barely whispered. "Hold it like this." His expression changed and I could see that he understood.

I took my thumb off the stem plug and he put his thumb on it, as I let him take the apple. He smiled and said, "Boy, that's a good lookin' apple. I'll save it for later."

He kept the apple tightly in his hand as we talked. Funny, it didn't look quite as guilty in his hand as it had in mine, but it still worried me.

"Don't look so worried, son." he said quietly. "It's gonna be okay." He didn't seem nervous at all. "I really appreciate this, Ronnie. I know it wasn't exactly easy for you to do it." I just stood there pushing a little rock around with my foot.

"Well, I just hope it helps you with your rings, July." I said after awhile. "But.....please don't get in trouble with it." I just kept looking at the ground and fiddling with that little rock.

"Don't you trust me, son?" he asked. I looked up at him for a few seconds. "Course I do, July." I said. "I just don't want you to get caught with it."

He bent down, put his hand on my shoulder and looked me in the eye. "Don't worry, son." he said. "You can trust me. Nothing bad is going to happen." He seemed to mean it. "Okay, July." I said. "I believe you."

"Well, I gotta get back to school. I don't want to be late and have to stay after school." I turned around and started walking away.

He called to me, "Thanks for the apple, Ronnie. Sure is a beauty."

On the way back to school, I felt relieved and even a little elated that I had actually had the nerve to do it. I ran all the way back, but every now and then, I still got that nagging, queasy feeling again. But, July had looked me in the eye and said that it would be okay and I believed him.

When I got home, I jumped up on the porch and hit the door with my shoulder as I turned the knob. The front door of this old house was one of those really heavy, wide ones - half again as wide as a modern front door and there was a row of four little windows that ran up and down on each side of it. That's the way they made them in the early eighteen hundreds when this house was built. The door was so big, I usually had to hit it with my shoulder to help me get it open.

I could hear my mom talking to someone in the living room. I

went in to see who was there and saw that she was only talking to

somebody on the phone. She seemed distressed at what she was

hearing and when she answered whoever it was, I could understand

why.

"Last night?...you mean he's dead? Where? Who else was there?

My God. ...and they all saw him do it? Yes...it's hard to believe.

Alright...I'll call the others...and tell them...but it won't be easy.

O.K....thanks for calling." She hung up the phone and looked at

me with a bewildered look. "Who's dead?" I asked. After a

moment she said, "Mr. Ramey....Ed Ramey."

"What happened to him?" I asked. She seemed a little dazed by

the whole thing. "Someone...shot him." "Why? What

happened?" I asked again. She just looked at me for a few seconds

and said, "I can't talk to you about this now. You're too young.

I'll tell you about it later." She left the room and I stood there wondering what that was all about.

The next day, I had to take my bicycle to Casey's welding shop to get it fixed. There was a place just outside town called "Hoot Owl Mountain".

The road up "Hoot Owl" was a mile or two of very steep, very narrow and very curvy road. We would push our bikes up to the top and then coast back down to the bottom. By the time you had gone a few hundred yards from the top, you were doing 40-50 miles an hour and after trying to slow down for a few of the curves, your brakes were so hot they were pretty well shot.

There was no way to stop until you got to the bottom, unless you hit a tree or something. At the bottom, there was a river and a one lane steel bridge with a rough wooden floor.

If there was a car coming across the bridge and using up the one lane, there was nothing to do but go beside the bridge into the river as some of my friends had done. If you were lucky enough to be able to go across the bridge, the impact of hitting those rough boards at that speed on a bicycle was a little like going up at 50 miles an hour on a freight elevator and having a 200 pound weight dropped on your shoulder at the same time. When I had hit that bridge a few days before, I heard a loud pop and I felt the bike give.

After I was able to stop, I looked over the bike to see what had happened. The frame was cracked in two places. Lucky for me, it didn't come completely apart or I would have been sliding across that bridge on my belly.

Anyway, I took the bike to Casey's welding shop to see if he could fix it. He had a sign over his door that said, "I can mend anything but a broken heart or a hole in the sky." He looked at the bike and said, "How in the world did you do this?" I told him and he just laughed and shook his head.

"Can you fix it?" I asked. "Sure I can," he said. "How much will it cost?" I asked. "Bout $200.00." he said. "$200.00!" I said, in disbelief.

He broke into a big smile, scratched his head and said, "Well, maybe since it's you, we could do it for..... how about a dollar?" I started to grin too, when I saw that he had been kidding me. "Okay," I said. "That'll be fine." I had about $1.25 in change in my pocket.

He gave me some dark goggles to put on so I could watch him weld it. I was fascinated as I watched the welding rod melt and fuse with the bike frame. I took the goggles off as soon as I could and looked at it. It was still almost white hot and smoking. I could feel the intense heat coming from it.

"How long will it take it to dry, Casey?" I asked. He looked at me and laughed. "Dry?" he asked.   "Nothing was ever any drier than that is right now. It doesn't dry, it cools." He splashed some cold water on it to cool it down.

"Don't ride it home....push it and stay off it for awhile." "Okay, Casey." I said, as I pulled out my pocket full of change and started counting out $1.00.

"Just put that money back in your pocket." he said. "This time it's on the house, but the next time, it'll cost you $200.00."

The leaves were beginning to change colors now and occasionally it was a little chilly at night. As beautifully green and rugged as the mountains were in the spring and summer, it always amazed me how brown and stark they became in the fall and winter. They looked almost burned.

It always depressed me....but not for long. Of course, when the

cool weather came, I had to wear my wool jacket. I really hated it.
It didn't look too bad, but I always felt as though I had prickly heat
when I had it on. If I got caught in the rain and got it a little wet, it
smelled sort of like a wet dog, but it kept me warm.

The house we lived in was a little frame house and like most
houses that were built before the Civil War, it was sturdy but not
very warm in the winter. I could always see my frosty breath when
I woke up on those cold mornings. I could also usually hear the
dogs barking under the house.

I really loved dogs and I had a habit of taking in every stray dog
that came along. They would usually stay under the house. There
wasn't much space under there, just a couple of feet of crawl space,
between the hand hewn beams and the ground. In some places, if
there was a small rise in the ground, the space between the beams
and the ground was less than a foot.

98.

A mother dog had been hanging around for a few days. Of course, I fed her and she crawled under the house and had her pups. I could hear the pups moaning and complaining that night, so I knew that she had had them. The next day, I crawled under there with some rags for them to sleep on and some food for the mother dog.

It was a tight squeeze in places and I got filthy doing it, but it was worth it to see the pups. She had eight and they were fat and healthy. I was amazed that she could have that many. She wasn't a big dog.

The next night, I woke up with a start in the middle of the night. I could hear a strange heaving sound under the floor. It was loud and getting louder. It was so regular and loud, it sounded almost like a machine. I sat up and listened for awhile. Then I got up and ran to the window.

It was pitch dark outside and all I could see was the eerie glowing

light of the fire flies, hanging in the air, flickering on and off like
Christmas lights.

I stood at the window, listening, trying to figure out what to do. I
decided to get the flashlight and go out and see if I could see
anything under the floor. The noise was becoming louder and
faster and more desperate. I jerked on my pants and grabbed my
jacket.

As I slid into my shoes and started into the kitchen to get the
flashlight - the noise suddenly stopped - just stopped, completely.
Everything was totally quiet. I went back to the window and
listened for awhile. It was as though the whole thing had been a
bad dream.

I got the flashlight anyway and went out to have a look under the
floor. I couldn't see anything at all and I wasn't about to crawl
under there at 2 o'clock in the morning. So, I went back to bed.

The next morning, I went out and very cautiously crawled under the floor. As I turned the corner past the bottom of the chimney, I saw something that really startled me. There, wedged between the ground and a beam was a huge bulldog.

Evidently, he had tried to get over to where the mother dog and pups were and had gotten himself wedged in so tightly that he couldn't get out and he had suffocated. He really looked horrible. His eyes were bulging and his tongue was hanging out. I didn't want to touch him, but I knew I couldn't leave him there. I reluctantly touched his leg. He was as stiff as a board. I tried for quite awhile to pull him out, but he was wedged in there as tight as a drum.

I had to get the shovel from the coal pile behind the house and dig out enough ground underneath him so that I could pull him out.

After I got him outside, I wasn't sure what to do with him. I knew

I had to bury him, but it occurred to me that he might have rabies. Then I had another sickening thought. If he did have rabies, I didn't know whether or not he had had any contact with the mother or any of her pups. In those days getting your dog vaccinated for rabies wasn't mandatory. So, most people didn't do it and every year there were a few rabid dogs.

I called my Mom out to have a look at him. She wasn't too happy with the way he looked either. "How can I tell if he's got rabies?" I asked. "I don't know." she said. "He doesn't seem to have been frothing at the mouth, but that doesn't mean he didn't have rabies. Let me call the Health Department and see if they can tell us what to do."

After awhile she came back out with a worried look on her face. "There's only one way to find out." She hesitated for a moment. It wasn't easy for her to say this. "You have to.....cut off his head and send it to the state capital. They can test it for rabies at the

Health Department there, but there's nobody here that can do it."

We just stood there and looked at each other for awhile. "There's no other way?" I asked. She slowly shook her head, no. "They have to have his head." she said. "Because they have to examine his brain. That's the only way they can tell. No other part of his body will do." "O.K." I said reluctantly. "Oh, one more thing." she said. "They said to be careful when you do it. Wear gloves and a mask, because even his saliva or his blood can infect you if he's got rabies." Just thinking about it gave me the creeps. There was never anything I wanted to do less, but I had to find out if he had rabies.

My Mom found out from the Health Department how we should package it. They said to wrap it in tin foil, pack it in dry ice before putting it in the box and to mark it Rush-Perishable.

I buried the rest of him down on the creek bank. No one ever mailed a grislier package and it took me a long time to shake the awful feeling the whole thing had given me. Then, of course, we had to wait a few days to find out what the results were. The thought of what we would have to do with the mother and pups, if the results were positive, was more than I could bring myself to even think about.

Finally, a few days later, the letter came. I was almost afraid to see what it had to say. My Mom opened it and looked at it for awhile. Then she looked at me and after a few seconds, she smiled. "He didn't have rabies." she said. I was so relieved, I could hardly speak.

I started out the door. "Where are you going?" she asked. I'm going down to see the pups." I said, on my way out. I had been staying away from them, except for leaving food for the mother, until we found out for sure about the test. That day, I played with all of them for a long time.

The pups grew fast. I gave away seven and kept one for myself. The mother dog stayed too. During the time that all the pups were still there, I had fourteen dogs. The mother dog and her eight pups plus five other grown dogs were all living there. After I had given away the seven pups, I still had seven dogs.

My Mom gave me another lecture about it. "Ronnie, this is ridiculous." "This place is almost like a kennel around here. It's getting so you can hardly sleep some nights for the barking. Don't take in any more strays. I'm not kidding this time." "But, Ma, I hate to turn 'em away hungry." I said. "I know you do." she said, "But you're going to have to, because if you feed them, they stay."

In the schoolyard, a few days later, I saw some boys I knew playing a game of marbles. I had a few marbles and a "steelie" in my pocket. A "steelie" was just a ball bearing about the size of a marble, but they were usually worth about five marbles.

I walked over and watched them play for a minute or so. Then I asked if I could get in the game. One of them said, "In a few minutes." As I was watching, one of the boys looked over his shoulder at me. "Did you hear what that nigger convict did?" he asked. "What do you mean?" I asked. It was his turn to shoot.

He took his time, made his shot and missed. He looked back at me with a sarcastic smile on his face. He knew I really wanted to know what he was talking about, but he wasn't going to tell me until I asked again. "What happened?" I asked again.

"Wouldn't you like to know?" he said. "What happened, damn it?" I said. "Alright, smart ass. One of them damn niggers stabbed a guard." he said. He seemed almost as though he was happy about it. "He didn't kill him, but not because the son of a bitch didn't try." I stood there stunned. "What do you think of them black bastards now?" he said.

I was still having trouble taking it all in. Finally, I was able to stammer almost inaudibly, "What was his name?" "Whose name?" he asked. "The convict's name." I said meekly. "His name?" he said laughing. "They ain't got no names. They're just nigger convicts. They've got numbers, but they ain't got no names. He was just a nigger with a knife. They're still tryin' to figure out where he got the knife. What the hell do you care, anyway?"

I hit him in the mouth as hard as I could. When I hit him, I lost my balance, spun around and fell down. He fell down too and started crying and holding his bleeding lip.

One of the other boys jumped on my chest and started hitting me in the face. I tried to hit him back, but he had my arms pinned. When he finished that, he got up and kicked me and they both ran. For a moment, my anger at the first boy and his foul mouth had pushed aside my horror at what he had told me. I laid there for awhile, then I slowly got up.

107.

Suddenly, everything he had said rushed back and it was overwhelming. I walked away in a daze. I couldn't go back to class feeling this way. I found a place between some trees and sat down on the ground and cried. Trying to figure out what to do now was agony. I didn't know if I should admit that I had given him the knife or say nothing and hope nobody found out.

That night, my Mom had already found out that I wasn't in class that afternoon. "Why weren't you in class and why were you fighting today. "He called me some names and I hit him." I said. "After that, I didn't feel like going back to class." She looked at me for a few seconds. I had several bruises on my face.

"Don't let it happen again." she said. "What's the matter with you?" she asked. I didn't say anything, so she asked again. "What's wrong with you?" "I'm just not feeling good, Ma." I said. She studied me a little longer and said, "Then go to bed."

108.

I laid there in bed trying to figure out what to do. I felt so
cowardly for not just admitting that I gave him the knife, but I was
scared to death to find out what would happen if I did tell the truth.
I felt awful for July, too. "Red Dog" must have done something
pretty bad, to get to him like that. I remembered what July said,
"Bad things can happen when there's nobody around to see".
Well, it was done now. If I had just refused to give him the knife,
he would be getting out in a few months.

Now, they would probably keep him for another ten years. Worse
still, they might even give him life. Then, of course, there was
"Red Dog". I didn't know how badly he was hurt, but I was
hoping that he wouldn't die.

It was all just too much for me to think about any more. I had to
sleep and try to get relief from it. Maybe things would look a little
better in the morning, but I had a strong feeling that they wouldn't.

I could hear the radio playing as I woke up the next morning. My Mom had a radio in the kitchen and she was listening while she fixed breakfast. As I walked into the kitchen, she looked around and said, "Would you like some juice?" "Sounds good." I said.

While I was drinking the orange juice, I sat there looking at that old yellow plastic radio. It had a sort of grill on the front of it that looked a little like the front end of a 1941 Studebaker.

The record that was playing ended and the announcer started reading the news. He read several stories about what was happening around the world and then he switched to the local news.

"A negro convict, who was working on the Slate Creek road crew, is being held in the county jail in connection with the stabbing of Rufus Delroy Turner, the head prison guard in charge of the road gang. The guard is in critical condition, but is expected to live."

"In the meantime, the convict will be held in solitary confinement, for his own protection, until his arraignment on Wednesday, on a charge of attempted murder. In further news…….." His voice trailed off as I thought about what he had said. I must have looked pretty worried when my Mom finally broke my daze. "Is there something bothering you?" she asked.

"What does arraign... ment mean?" I asked. I had some trouble saying the word. "Arrangement?" she asked. "No arraign ... ment." I said. "Like in court."

"Oh, you mean like that convict they were talking about on the radio?" she said. "Yes." I said. "Well, an arraignment is what they call the court proceeding in which they officially charge someone with a crime. Then the actual trial comes later." "Will he be there?" I asked. "Who?" she asked. "The convict." I said.

"Yes, of course, he will be there." she replied. "Can people go and

watch that?" I asked. "Yes." she said, "There are usually
spectators for arraignments."

"Why are you so interested in that?" she asked.

I sat there for awhile looking at the dregs of the orange juice in my
glass. I came very close to telling her about the knife right then,
but I just couldn't bring myself to do it.

"Oh, no reason," I said after a moment. "It's just interesting.
That's all." "Are you sure you're alright?" she asked. "I'm fine." I
said.

For the next few days, I was pretty worthless. In school, the
teachers were constantly yelling at me for not paying attention and
for not doing my homework. At home, my Mom was still asking
me what was wrong with me. I tried to act normal, but I felt as
though I was standing on a trap door waiting for the bottom to drop
out. Finally, Wednesday rolled around.

112.

At recess that morning, I ran over to the courthouse, which was only a few blocks away. I had been in there a few times before.

It was a great old three story stone building with a clock tower. There was a big clock face on each of the four sides of the tower and it chimed every hour. You could hear it all over town.

The whole town had been built around this courthouse. It was built in 1858. The Civil War had marched and struggled and limped past these windows and some of it had gotten stuck here.

I didn't know where I should go after I got inside and I was gawking at everything in the place. There was a lot to see. It smelled like cigars.

One of the guards there saw me walking down the hall and stopped me. I knew this guard. In a town as small as that, everybody knows everybody. Besides, there was something rather unusual about this particular guard.

113.

Everybody said he had an, "unforgettable smile". As soon as you saw him, you understood what they meant. When he opened his mouth, it got everybody's attention. You might even say that the room sort of lit up when he smiled, because every tooth in his head was gold. It made him look very strange and a little scary.

Why he wanted to have that done, I don't know. Some people said he thought it made him look prosperous. Actually, it made his dentist look prosperous. "What are you doin' here, Ronnie?" he asked. "Shouldn't you be in school?" I was just wonderin' when that arraign ..…ment was gonna be?" I said. "What arraignment?" he asked.

"The one for the convict." I said. "You mean that nigger?" he said. "Well, that ain't till about two o'clock this afternoon. What do you want to know about it?"

"Just when it's gonna be, that's all." I said.

114.

He gave me a funny look as he watched me walk away and out the door. I ran back to school and got back to class late. When they let us out for the afternoon recess, I was on my way back to the courthouse and I knew I wouldn't be going back to school that day.

By the time I got back to the courthouse and up to the courtroom, the procedure was already in progress. The same guard that I had talked to that morning saw me come into the back of the room and he came over to me.

"What are you doin' here again? I know you're supposed to be in school now," he said. I knew he was going to hassle me.

"It's for a class project." I said. "I'm supposed to watch it so I can tell the class about it." He studied me for a few seconds over the rims of his glasses. "Alright." he said. "But you better be quiet and not cause no trouble back here." "I promise." I said. "I won't cause any trouble."

115.

Since I was in the back of the room and was pretty short, I couldn't
see too much over the heads of the other people. I could see the
judge in his elevated chair and I could see a fat man in a suit that
was too tight for him, standing up and talking to the judge.

I couldn't see July, but I knew he was sitting up there somewhere.
The whole thing made me very nervous, maybe because I felt as
though I should be up there, being charged too, since I had
supplied the weapon.

I was still straining my neck trying to see July, but I just couldn't. I
was at the very back of the courtroom and there was nobody sitting
behind me. Since there was nobody looking at me from behind, I
got down on the floor and looked under the seats. After a few
seconds, I spotted a pair of rough work shoes like the ones the
convicts wore.

His feet were chained together at the ankles. It really made me sad to see the chains. Now he was chained just like the worst men on the chain gang. Last week, he was a trustee and now he was chained and being charged with attempted murder. All because of my stupidity.

As I got back up in my seat, I could see the judge looking at me. It occurred to me that maybe if I explained to the judge, that I gave July the knife, they might go easier on him. I meekly raised my hand.

The judge looked at the guard and nodded toward me. The guard gave me the sternest look he could muster. With those teeth it was pretty easy. I put my hand down.

The fat man in the small suit, who had been talking, finally sat down and another man got up and talked for awhile. I didn't understand a lot of what they were saying, but it sounded pretty serious.

117.

Finally, the judge said, "Obviously, there will be no bail, since the man is already a prisoner. He will be held in the county jail, in solitary confinement, for his own protection, until his trial date, which will be......."

He looked over his glasses at his assistant, who looked in a book for a few seconds and then told the judge a date.

The judge repeated the date and said, "That will be in three weeks. Court's adjourned." Then he hit the desk with his gavel. The guard said, "All rise." Everybody got up, so I stood up too. Then the judge got up and left.

Everybody stood there for awhile and then they started milling around. I still couldn't see July. With everybody standing up, I could see even less than before.

Suddenly, I could hear a rattling sound over the murmur of the voices. It was the ankle chains rattling as the guards led him out of the room. Then, for just an instant, there was a small break in the wall of people in front of me and I got a glimpse of the guards and their prisoner.

As he came into view, it was almost like slow motion. When I saw his face, I couldn't believe it. <u>It wasn't July!!</u>

It was "Big Jake", the big man with the sledge hammer and the far away look. The one July said was already doing life. I was stunned. How could this be? My mind was racing. <u>It wasn't July!!</u>

Somehow I managed to get out of the courthouse and onto the street. It felt as though it was all a dream. I ran home as fast as I could and got on my bike.

I don't think I ever rode it as fast as I did that day, on my way up Slate Creek to where the convicts were working. When I got to the top of the hill overlooking the work crew, I looked around for July.

Finally, I spotted him standing on top of a huge boulder about fifty yards away, drawing one of his maps of the terrain on a little brown piece of paper. He was lost in thought.

It was too late in the day for me to talk to him anyway. They had already had their afternoon break. I just had to see for myself that he was really there. As I turned around to start back, he looked up and saw me.

He gave me a sort of quizzical look for a second. I suppose he was wondering why I hadn't been around for a few days. Then he put his arm up and waved a broad wave. I waved back with the broadest wave I could.

Then I started home. I knew my Mom was going to be mad at me for missing school that afternoon, but I wasn't worried about that. The only thing that worried me now was whether or not July still had the knife I had given him.

But for now, it was enough just to know he didn't do what I thought he had done. That night, I got the best night's sleep I had had in a long time.

The next morning, I almost bounced out of bed. I was feeling so good that I didn't even mind standing in line waiting for my typhoid booster shot at school. I remembered that I had missed my last booster shot the year before, but I didn't figure it mattered.

One of the reasons they always gave us for taking the shots was that swimming in the river without having the shots was really dangerous. The river was badly polluted. Most of the time, the water looked like ink because of all the run off from the coal mines. I swam in the river all the time. If you wanted to swim, that's where you had to do it.

There were a few other streams around there besides Slate Creek, that ran into the big Levisa River. One of them was the Dismal

River. It was a smaller river and it was only a few miles away. So, sometimes we would go swimming there, because it was a little cleaner, though not much, than the Levisa. Dismal was the actual name of the river and the place it ran through was known as Dismal.

A lot of places around there had sad sounding names like that. As you came down the road that ran along beside the Levisa, there were places with names like Grimsleyville, Contrary Creek, Dismal and a few others with similar sounding names.

On the Dismal River there was a place where we used to swim that had a big cliff hanging out over the water. We called it, "Hangin' Rock". We would usually jump off the cliff into the water, but there was also a big oak tree that grew on top of the cliff, which could give you a little more height, if you wanted it, when you jumped in. You just had to be careful to jump out far enough, so you wouldn't hit the edge of the cliff on the way down.

When you hit the water, you usually hit pretty hard and went down fairly deep and you couldn't see much, because the water was so murky from all the coal slag and other pollution that ran into it.

One day, I had just jumped in the water and when I came up I heard my friend Jerry Davis, who was still up on the cliff, yelling – "Look out - to your left!" I looked off to my left and there was a big water moccasin, which is a very poisonous snake, swimming toward me. He was about ten or fifteen feet from me and moving fast.

I guess I had startled him when I jumped in and he was going to get me for it. I don't think I ever swam that fast in my life, before or after that. I must have looked like a torpedo, that was leaving a wake the size of a paddle wheel. I got back on the bank in record time and watched the big snake, to see if he was going to come out of the water after me. He didn't.

Little did I know that another kind of snake, as deadly as that water moccasin, had already bitten me in that water. But, it was going to wait awhile before it tried to kill me.

We all swam there many, many times over the years. I suppose we should have seen the danger from all the pollution, but none of us ever dreamed that we could get sick from it. At that age, we all thought we were immortal anyway.

Finally, it was my turn in line to get my shot. They gave us the shots right before lunch. As soon as they let us out for lunch, I started up the road to see July. All the way up there I was trying to come up with some way of putting it all together, so I could tell him about what I thought had happened. I was also thinking about all the good things I knew about July.

124.

There was just something about him that set him apart from the other men. They all seemed to sense that difference and they trusted him and trust was a rare thing in that group. I guess they saw his strength and honest decency.

They all knew that he had been through some of the worst of it and he was still strong. He hadn't let it destroy him. If anything, it had made him stronger and wiser. He had become more, rather than less. He had survived without compromise and they all respected him for that. They looked up to him and he never abused that trust. I trusted him too.

I should have remembered all these things and I should have known he couldn't have done a thing like that. I just panicked and figured the whole thing all wrong. But, there was still the knife.

I found him sitting on a tree stump eating his lunch. When he saw me coming, he asked the guard if he could talk to me.

The guard nodded. July seemed really glad to see me and I was glad to see him.

"Where you been, boy? I ain't talked to you in a week or so. I thought you'd forgotten about me. When I saw you yesterday, I thought maybe you was mad or somethin'."

"No, I didn't forget about you, July," I said, "and I'm not mad." I stood there for a moment trying to figure out the best way to explain it all. "I didn't think you were here, July." I said finally. He gave me an incredulous look and laughed. "Didn't think I was here?" he said. "Well now, where else do you think I could be? I don't think the guards would like it too much if I left."

"No." I said. "I mean I thought you were the one who…" I was fumbling for the right words. "The one who stabbed the guard." I whispered. His smile faded and he got a very puzzled look on his face.

"What made you think…..Oh…..because of the knife." he said in a half whisper. "Have you still got it, July?" I asked. I could see his disappointment at that question.

For some reason, I was really starting to sweat. After a moment, he said, "Yes, I've still got it." He looked around to see if the guard was looking. The guard wasn't looking at us. July put his foot up on a stump and started scratching his ankle. "Look down here, Ronnie."

I looked down at his ankle and he pulled back his sock a little and showed me the knife. It was in his sock and slightly down inside his high top work shoe. I felt really badly that I had even asked him about it. My sweating was getting worse.

"I'm sorry, July. I should have trusted you, like you told me to." He just looked at me for a moment without saying anything. Then he said, "It's all right, Ronnie, I understand."

"I would probably have thought the same thing." Then he put his hand on my shoulder and said, "But you do understand now….that you can trust me, don't you, son?"

"I told you I figured out a long time ago that old "Red Dog" could ruin my life if I let him. God knows he tried hard enough to get me to lose my temper, but I never let him do it. This time he finally pushed the wrong man too far. "Big Jake" had nothin' to lose. "Red Dog" is lucky he's still breathin'."

"This knife ain't gonna hurt nobody." he said. I was having trouble looking him in the eye. "I do understand, July and I'm sorry. I feel stupid for thinking that."

"Don't feel stupid, boy, because you ain't. Anyway, let's forget about that. I got some real good news to tell you."

I could see he was really happy about something and anxious to tell me about it. "What is it?" I asked. He held back for a few seconds, savoring the good news. "Come on, July, what is it?"

Finally, he really lit up and said, "I'm gettin' out .... in two weeks! They're lettin' me out three weeks early, 'cause I'm a trustee!" The smile on my face must have stretched from ear to ear. "That's great, July! God, that's fantastic!" "It sure is." he said. "On October 16th, I'll be on that 10:00 o'clock bus to Bluefield."

All the bad things seemed eons ago now. We just stood there laughing together. Laughing hard. It was a good moment. But, as we were laughing, I started feeling dizzy. July looked at me and said, "You alright, Ronnie? You don't look too good." "No." I said. "I'm feeling a little dizzy."

Now things were beginning to look sort of green to me.

"I think .... I'm getting' sick, July." "What caused this?" he asked. "I don't know." I said. "But I think it's gettin' worse. I feel really sick."

He bent down and looked at me and put his hand on my forehead. "You're burnin' up, Ronnie. You better get home fast. I'd help you if I could, but there ain't nothin' I can do for you here."

"I'm goin'." I said. I turned around and started back toward school. I was feeling sicker by the second. I half turned to July. He looked really worried. "Go on Ronnie, quick, before it gets any worse."

"I'm goin'." I said again. Now I was sweating worse than ever and feeling sick at my stomach. I started walking faster but I was having trouble walking in a straight line. I was staggering and weaving. By the time I got within sight of the school, which seemed to take forever, I could hardly walk.

I stopped and threw up several times. I finally made it to the schoolyard before I passed out. When I woke up, I was still in a half daze, but now I was inside somewhere. There were people standing over me and I felt sicker than ever. Then everything went black again.

The next time I woke up, I was in my own bed at home. My Mom was looking at me and Dr. Ripley was sitting beside the bed. I don't think he knew I was awake. I could barely open my eyes and my vision was very fuzzy, but I could see him sitting there. He was writing something on a little white pad. I remember thinking what a good man he was and how much I liked him. He had always taken care of my minor ailments and injuries. I couldn't remember a time when I hadn't known him.

I was so weak I could hardly move, but I could hear him talking to my Mom. "Gladys, he's got typhoid. You'll have to keep him in bed for at least a couple of weeks. Evidently, he already had it in his system and the typhoid shot at school caused a violent reaction. I think he'll probably survive it, but he's got to have complete rest and lots of fluids, or at least as much as he can keep down. Get this prescription filled and give him those the way I wrote it there. I'll be back tomorrow."

Then I felt myself drifting off again. I didn't really care about anything. I just wanted to sleep. For the next seven or eight days, I was slightly more than a vegetable. Just slightly more. I must have lost fifteen pounds and I probably only weighed 65 or 70 pounds to begin with. Most of the time, I didn't know if I was alive or dead and I didn't much care.

My temperature was so high, I felt as though my brain had been fried. I could barely keep even a glass of water down and I must have thrown up in a bucket at least a hundred times. I was also having horrible nightmarish dreams.

Then, after that first few days I at least stopped throwing up and my temperature went down to a few degrees above normal. For the next few days, the most I could do was lie there.

I tried to get up by myself a couple of times, but my legs buckled and I fell back on the bed, exhausted. I couldn't even make it as far as the bathroom without my Mom's help. Dr. Ripley came by every day.

By the time I had been in bed for twelve or thirteen days, I was getting some of my strength back. I still felt very weak, but I was feeling much better, even though I must have looked like one of the living dead.

About six o'clock that evening, my Mom brought me in a bowl of vegetable soup and some crackers. I was really hungry and I could hardly wait to eat.

"How are you feeling?" she asked. "A lot better." I said. "I'm hungry. Everything still tastes a little like glue, but at least I can keep it down now." She seemed pleased. "I'm glad you're hungry."

133.

"A few days ago you couldn't even look at food." I nodded. "That reminds me." I said. "Have you been feeding the dogs?" "Of course," she said. "Are you sure they're getting enough? I don't want them to be hungry." "Don't worry about it." she said. "They haven't missed a meal. They're eating better than you are." We both laughed. "They're not sick." I said.

"Is Dr. Ripley coming back tomorrow?" I asked. "I talked to him before he left this afternoon." she said. "He said the sixteenth would be a very busy day for him, so he'll be by later than usual." "The sixteenth?" I asked.

"Yes." she said. "Tomorrow is the sixteenth." "The sixteenth of what?" I asked. "Of October." she said. "You've lost track of everything."

"I sure have." I said. "The sixteenth." I thought. My God, I didn't realize how long it had been since all this began.

134.

After I finished the soup and crackers, she took the dishes back into the kitchen. The local paper, which came out every Wednesday, was lying there just within reach, if I stretched my arm a little.

I was pretty bored, so I pulled it over and started reading it. My vision was still a little blurry, but I could make out most of what it said, so I started reading it. There was a story about Burt Loggins.

I had seen him a few times. He was a tall rawboned looking man with narrow set eyes and a big mustache. He had made a lot of money in the coal mining business. He scared me a little, because he always looked as though he was mad at somebody. Besides, I'd heard that he carried a gun.

It seems he was playing poker with some of his friends, when they started arguing about something. Things went really sour and Mr. Loggins pulled out a gun and shot Ed Ramey who was sitting across from him - point blank. Mr. Ramey was dead before he hit the floor.

Burt Loggins was arrested and charged with murder. He was out on bail the same day. There was a trial two months later and even though there were four witnesses who saw him do it, he was acquitted on all charges.

As I read this, I realized that this was what my mother was hearing on the phone that day, a couple of months ago. They must have had the trial during these weeks I'd been laid up.

Even to my eleven year old mind, there was a big difference in the way justice, or what passed for it, got meted out in the eyes of that little piece of the world.

Then another story suddenly caught my eye and a shock went through me - the name Culler was in it. I couldn't believe it. I read it as fast as I was able too. It said, "according to testimony

136.

from guards, convict July Culler - at some risk to himself - had probably prevented the death of head guard R.D. Turner, by talking the man with the knife into stopping before things got any worse."

My God, July hadn't said a word about any of this when I talked to him about it. He had saved "Red Dog's" life and he didn't even mention it.

I couldn't sit still and I could hardly wait to tell my Mom that I knew July. I was hoping she would come back from the kitchen soon, so I could tell her how proud and amazed I was at what he had done.

I really felt more energy than I had in weeks, but I could feel it ebbing. I knew I was still too weak to get up. I called to her, but I guess she couldn't hear me. I guess she had taken out the garbage or something.

She was taking forever. I laid back and was planning to wait until she got back. I tried to stay awake, but I just couldn't. I could feel myself dozing. Then, I nodded off again. I don't know how long I slept, but I suddenly woke up with a start. "The sixteenth!" I thought. "That was the day July said he was getting out." I tried hard to remember what he had said. It all seemed so muddled in my mind.

I knew he said the sixteenth, but he also said something else. Something about Bluefield. I just couldn't remember. My mind was mush and it was really frustrating. I kept going over it till I finally got totally disgusted with myself for not being able to remember.

My Mom had put the old yellow plastic radio from the kitchen on the table beside my bed. I turned it on and listened for awhile. They played some music, then did some news, then more music. I didn't like most of the music they were playing.

A commercial for a furniture store came on. They were talking about new store hours or something, starting at 10:00 o'clock in the morning.

Then the bad music started again. I would have changed the station but there wasn't a great selection to choose from. After about five minutes, they did the same furniture store commercial again. While I was lying there, half listening, they must have read that commercial about every five or ten minutes for the next half hour. It was really annoying.

After I had heard it about six times, it finally clicked. When the announcer said 10:00 o'clock in the morning, I remembered.

"That's what July said." I thought. "I'll be on the 10:00 o'clock bus….to Bluefield." That was it. I woke up several times that night, thinking about it. Was I right? Was that really what he said? It seemed right.

My Mom had been working full time again now that I was getting

better. She went to work every morning and then dropped in to

check on me several times a day. So, I was alone most of the

morning.

Before she left the next morning, she came into my room and

looked at me. I opened my eyes. "Will you be alright?" she asked.

"I'll be fine." I said. "What time is it?" "It's eight thirty." she said.

"I'll see you in a few hours."

As soon as she was out the door, I started trying to get up and it

wasn't easy. Getting dressed and going outside seemed like a large

job to me. I knew I had to start getting ready right away or I'd

never make it in time. Everything I did seemed incredibly slow

and I was having trouble finding my clothes, since I hadn't worn

anything but pajamas in two weeks.

I was still so weak I could feel the sweat popping out all over me, just from trying to do something as simple as getting dressed. By the time I was finally ready to go, it was 9:15 and I still had to walk the two blocks to the bus station. It seemed like two miles to me. The sun seemed blinding. I stopped a couple of times and rested a few seconds. At last, I could see the bus station up ahead.

When I got to the window, I cupped my hands on the dirty glass so I could see inside. I spotted July standing way over in the corner, away from everybody else. He was standing there in a wrinkled $20.00 suit and his old Stetson hat, with his bag of rings in his hand. It was everything he had in the world. You could see that he was scared. For the first time in ten years, he was on his own again and he knew he was totally vulnerable to the dangers and whims of anybody who happened to want to take advantage of him or use him as a scapegoat. They could even use the legal system to do it.

He knew he was not in a safe place. It was only safe for him there as long as people thought of him as a convict, who was confined and guarded. Now things were different. Now he could be considered a threat. He knew he had to get out of there fast.

I went around to the door and walked in. When July saw me, he looked shocked. I must have looked like death itself. "My God, Ronnie, what happened? You look......bad. I was really worried about you and there wasn't any way I could find out." "I had typhoid, July." I said. "From swimmin' in the river, I guess."

"Typhoid?" he said with disbelief. "That coulda' killed you." "It almost did." I said. "That's why I look like this. But I'm almost over it now. I've just got to get my strength back. I'll be O.K. now."

We must have been an odd looking sight standing there. The only black man and the palest kid in town. A few people were looking at us partly for that reason and partly because some of them didn't like the fact that I was talking to him.

"Well, July, you made it. You're out!" "I sure am, Ronnie. It still
don't seem real to me. I guess it won't for quite awhile." We were
both laughing. There were a few people who didn't seem to like
that either.

"I was afraid I wasn't going to get here in time to say goodbye." I
said. "Well, I'm sure glad you did, son."

I didn't say anything for awhile. I was still trying to figure out
how to say this right. Finally, I just said it…."I heard about you
savin' "Red Dog's" life." He smiled. "Who told you that?" "I
read about it in the paper," I said.

"In the paper?" he said. He was shaking his head. He seemed
amazed and humbled that anyone would write something about
him in the paper. "Yep, it was all in the paper." I said.

"Well, maybe not all." he said. "It got pretty bad." "What happened?" I asked. He seemed to be trying to find the right words to explain it all. "I could see he was fixin' to finish off "Red Dog"….and when I tried to stop him, I thought he was gonna' kill me….he was wild."

"You didn't have to do what you did, July." I said. "You took a big chance." He smiled, then that faded. "Well, I just did what I thought I had to do. I figured if I could stop it and I didn't, I'd always be sorry….besides, it wasn't just "Red Dog's" life….it was "Big Jake's" life too. The guards were goin' to shoot him. I don't know if I done him a favor though. I think he wanted to die." "Well, I'm just glad I got the chance to tell you, July….I'm glad I know you….and I'm proud that you're my friend." "Thank you Ronnie. I won't forget that."

The man in the ticket booth yelled out, "Bluefield bus now loading."

I looked up at the clock. It said 9:50. July looked down at me and extended his hand. As we shook hands, he smiled and said, "Who would have thought that you and me would ever even know each other, Ronnie…much less that we'd be buddies?"

Then he said, "You already understand somethin' important that some people never figure out as long as they live. Don't forget that you know that." "I won't, July."

We heard the man in the ticket booth again, "Last call for Bluefield". "Well son, I guess I better be gittin' on the bus." he said slowly. "Yeah July, you don't want to miss this one. Where'll you go from Bluefield?"

"I can make connections in Bluefield that'll take me on out to Suffolk, where I was born," he said.

As he got on the bus, he turned and said, "You goin' to be O.K., Ronnie?"

"Sure July, I'll be O.K." He looked at me and smiled. "Yeah Ronnie, you're goin' to be O.K." Then he disappeared into the bus.

The bus driver was revving the engine and as he closed the big door, I saw July through the window as he sat down in the back of the old bus. The bus slowly lumbered out of the terminal and I could see July waving. I waved back. Thick dust curled up behind the bus as I watched it slowly go out of sight.

That was the last time I ever saw July, but I never forgot him. In the months that followed, "Big Jake" got twenty years added on to his sentence, as though it mattered, since he was doing life anyway. "Red Dog" recovered and I heard he got religion and retired.

The road job went on at the same grueling pace, just like it had been, for several months until the job was finished. They had to stop a few times because of heavy rain and snow. I went up and watched the road gang from a distance a couple of times, just to see how it was going, but that was as close as I got. I didn't have much interest in it after that. It just wasn't the same without July there. Sometimes you meet the best people in some of the most unexpected places.

Years later, while I was listening to Dr. King speaking on television, he quoted a man from the period right after the Civil War. The man was a former slave and had become a preacher.

He said:

> *"We ain't what we oughta be,*
> *we ain't what we wanta be,*
> *we ain't what we gonna be,*
> *but thank God, we ain't what we was."*

On that day, I was thinking of July Culler.

147.

He was a good man, one of the best I've ever known and I will always be glad I had the privilege of knowing him. I hope he found a good life out there somewhere - he deserved it.

Made in the USA
Charleston, SC
06 March 2014